STAR TREK II®
SHORT
STORIES

STAR TREK II® SHORT STORIES

by William Rotsler

WANDERER BOOKS
Published by Simon & Schuster, New York

STAR TREK® II SHORT STORIES
William Rotsler

Published by WANDERER BOOKS
A Simon & Schuster Division of Gulf & Western Corporation
Simon & Schuster Building
1230 Avenue of the Americas
New York, New York 10020
WANDERER and colophon are trademarks of Simon & Schuster

Designed by Stanley S. Drate

Manufactured in the United States of America

10 9 8 7 6 5 4 3 2 1

Library of Congress Cataloging in Publication Data

Rotsler, William.
  Star trek II short stories.

  Contents: The blaze of glory—Under twin moons—Wild Card—[etc.]
  1. Science fiction, American. 2. Children's stories,
American. [1. Science fiction. 2. Short stories]
I. Star trek, II, the wrath of Khan. II. Title.
III. Title: Star trek 2 short stories. IV. Title:
Star trek two short stories.
PZ7.R753St 1982   [Fic]   82-17558
ISBN 0-671-46390-X

For
BILL WARREN,
without whom life would
be much duller

Contents

The Blaze of Glory

Admiral James T. Kirk stepped from the sonic shower with a feeling of fresh excitement. In a matter of two hours they would drop out of warp speed and use their impulse engines to put them in orbit around Regulus III, the planet called Khepri. Then he would welcome aboard Fleet Admiral Karis Atum Tatenen, the hero of the Bottle of Vonra—the Destroyer of Klingons as the media had dubbed him.

Kirk looked at himself in the mirror, critically examining his still-youthful body. He was no longer the trim, brash young lieutenant who had shipped into space aboard the *Farragut*, but thanks to constant exercise, the longevity serum, and a good diet he was in reasonable shape.

No, blast it, he grinned, *good* shape!

Kirk quickly donned his dress uniform and took the turbolift to the bridge. As he entered Lieutenant Commander Sulu rose from the captain's chair. "Captain on the bridge," announced Sulu.

"I have the conn," Kirk said formally. He dropped into the familiar command chair as Sulu took the navigator's place. "ETA, Mister Sulu."

"Four minutes to subject, an estimate forty-two into stable orbit, sir."

Kirk punched the chair-arm control. "Engine Room."

"*Aye, sir!*"

"Scotty, everything ready?"

"*Aye, sir! The reception committee is suiting up now.*"

"Bridge out." Kirk looked at Uhura. "Mister Spock to the bridge, please."

She broadcast the request over the ship and in a few moments Commander Spock appeared, lean and almost satanic. "Admiral?"

"Spock, everything's all right?"

"If you mean for Admiral Tatenen's arrival, yes, sir. The main guest cabin is ready. The yeoman has the admiral's favorite beverages. We consulted the ship's computer and have programmed his favorite music."

"Good, good." Kirk looked at Spock and grinned slightly. "I don't mind telling you, Mister Spock, it's . . . it's like meeting Nelson or . . . or Drake. Tatenen is one of the greatest heroes in Federation history!"

"So I noted, Admiral. If I may say so, it might be comparable to me meeting Surak, the father of Vulcan logical thought—but on an entirely different level, of course."

"Yes, that would be more like me meeting Plato, or Bones meeting Hippocrates. Tatenen's quite old, of course. But still a serving officer," Kirk added hastily. "I remember reading his *Battle of Vonra* in the Academy and—"

Just then the *Enterprise* dropped out of warp speed and there lay Regulus. Sulu adjusted course and Khepri appeared dead ahead. Somewhere closer to its sun—which the natives called Ra and the Federation doggedly called Regulus—were Horus and Osiris. Further out were cold Khonsu and frigid Ptah. And even further out were the gas giant Rhamses and the iceball called Nefertari.

Kirk waited with ill-concealed impatience as the great cruiser moved gracefully into orbit. "Admiral Tatenen's party is ready to board, sir," Uhura announced.

"Sulu, take the conn," Kirk ordered. He and Spock left the bridge at once. In the main transporter room Kirk glanced at the double row of young lieutenants standing at attention, then nodded to the Transporter Chief. "Beam them aboard."

The columns of sparkling light appeared and became Fleet Admiral Tatenen and four of his staff. "Permission to come aboard, Admiral," Tatenen said in his powerful voice.

"Permission granted!" Kirk said, saluting the legend who stepped from the transporter bench. He was a tall, impressive man, white-haired with large physical features given to broad, almost theatrical, gestures.

Tatenen turned to the first of his staff. "Captain Tapia, my chief of staff," Kirk and Tapia exchanged firm handshakes. "Baroness Commander Amalia, my aide-de-camp." Kirk smiled as he exchanged greetings with the beautiful young woman—on whom the Federation uniform appeared to be painted.

"Commander Ogar and Lieutenant Commander Anderson," Tatenen said. "Off the stage," he commanded, gesturing. To the Transporter Chief he said, "Bring the rest of our gear up at once and have it appropriately stowed."

"Yessir!" the young officer snapped, plainly impressed.

"Now, Kirk, let's see this ship of yours, shall we? I have been hearing fantastic things about you. The V'ger affair, you must tell me everything, I'm dying to hear."

"Thank you, Admiral, I'd be most pleased, but . . ." He hesitated. "Your orders, sir. I was told you would provide the destination."

"Ah, of course. Baroness?" The blonde young woman pulled a small plastic block from the dispatch case which hung from her shoulder and handed it to Kirk. He looked at it, saw the imperial seal of the Emperor of Miradi on the information block. Kirk raised his eyebrows.

"A secret destination, Admiral?" Kirk asked. The dark plastic block was a molecular recording device which, when inserted into a ship's navigation computer and then activated, would direct the vessel to the device's encoded location. A simple computation, once underway, would give them the main direction, but one never knew when the course would be changed or, indeed, what the final destination was.

Admiral Tatenen put his arm around Kirk's shoulders. "Ah, don't you worry, son. You know how they use old duffers like me." He took Kirk out into the corridor and toward the turbolift, followed by Spock and the entourage. "Secret diplomacy, powers behind thrones, that sort of thing."

"But I might better be able to do the job if I know where—"

"In time, son, in time. Don't you worry. Just pop that cube in the nav computer and let's be on our way. Now you just show me this ship of yours, hey? Ogar, you watch things here."

As they entered the turbolift Kirk handed the cube to Spock. "Take care of this," he said, meaningfully looking his First Officer in the eye.

"Yes, Admiral," Spock responded.

"Anderson!" Admiral Tatenen said, "You get us settled down now, y'hear?"

"Yes, sir!" Anderson said in a calm voice. He remained with Spock as Kirk, Baroness Amalia, and Captain Tapia entered the turbolift.

"Show me the engine room first, son, and save the

bridge for last. I like the bridge best of all, y'know."
Kirk nodded, remembering reading of the devastated
bridge of the *King Richard*, air leaking out, half the
phasers out, warp engines ready to blow. But still
Tatenen had sent volley after volley into the Klingon
battleships which greatly outnumbered him.

Tatenen had won that battle, and many more after
that, against both Klingons and Romulans. But it had
been twenty-nine years before, almost seven decades
after the end of the Romulan War, when there had
been an attempt by that savage race to break the
treaty. Kirk wondered what the great admiral had
been doing since then. When he had received his
orders he was faintly surprised that the old man was
even still alive.

Kirk glanced at Baroness Amalia. She's a cool one,
he thought, but I must not misunderstand or misin-
terpret her relationship to Tatenen. They toured the
engine room and Tatenen spoke with generosity to a
beaming Montgomery Scott. They passed through
the rec room where the crew there broke into sponta-
neous applause, something Kirk had never seen happen before. He also noted that Tatenen did not seem
surprised.

I wonder what it must be like, Kirk thought, to be
immediately recognized wherever you go, to have
people applaud and admire. Some kings don't get
that, he thought, perhaps only the most famous and
beloved of entertainers.

Then they came upon the bridge. The people there
were too disciplined to applaud, but they cast admir-

ing glances at this most famous of star sailors. Kirk offered the command chair to Tatenen, but he refused.

"Thank you, no, son. If I took it I might just not give it back," he laughed. "Well, you certainly have a fine ship here, Admiral, a fine ship. I see the updating and retrofitting has done wonders. Excellent, excellent." He turned to Baroness Amalia. "Come, Commander, let's get to work on . . ." He paused and gave Kirk a wide smile and a wink. "Y'know, Admiral, I have to watch what I say. That's what I have Amalia here for, and she watches out for an old man's slips of the tongue." She merely smiled, a soft and, Kirk thought, a knowing smile.

Captain Tapia, who had been silent all through the inspection, spoke up. "Your Commander Spock, where is he?"

The turbolift hissed open and Spock entered. He nodded to Admiral Tatenen and strode over to hand the cube to Sulu. "Mister Sulu, this is your prepared course."

Sulu took the cube, saw the royal seal and glanced up at the impassive Spock. He peeled off the seal, the cube turned red, and he pressed it into the proper slot on his console. "Ready, sir."

"The gear all aboard, Spock?" Admiral Tatenen asked.

"Yes, Admiral."

"Let her rip, son," Admiral Tatenen said.

Sulu hesitated, glancing around at Kirk, who nodded. Sulu's expert fingers touched the studs and buttons, and the great ship came to life. The *feel* of the ship on impulse engines was totally different from the way it seemed on warp drive.

The *Enterprise* broke orbit and headed away. "Warp One," Admiral Tatenen said. "As soon as we hit that it'll all be automatic."

"Warp One, Mister Sulu," Kirk said.

The stars blurred and ran past as Admiral Tatenen looked at the big forward screen with a pleased expression. "I love this moment," he said.

"Admiral," the baroness said softly after a few moments.

"What? Oh. Oh, all right." He smiled at Kirk. "Don't ever get old, Admiral. They hound you to death. Better I should have signed off on the bridge of the *King Richard*." He slapped his stomach. "Wonder of modern science, Kirk. Practically nothing is what I was born with." He laughed and put his arm around the slim, beautiful baroness. "Very well, Amalia, let's go rummage around in the pills."

As he went into the turbolift, Tatenen called out to Kirk. "Given the opportunity, Admiral—go down with your ship! In the long run it's the best!"

The doors hissed closed and there was silence on the bridge, except for the mutter of navigation reports, the beep and pop of signals, and the deep thrum of the great matter-antimatter engines.

"Mister. Spock, I'd like to see you in my quarters in ten minutes," Kirk said. "Mister Sulu, you have the conn."

"Aye, sir." Sulu turned to watch Admiral Kirk

leave the bridge, and then he turned back to exchange another look with Commander Spock.

"I shall be in the captain's quarters," Spock said.

"All right, Mister. Spock, what was in that cube?"

"A devious course, Admiral, to Pollox IV."

"Pollox IV?" exclaimed Kirk. "That's disputed territory!"

"Exactly, sir. Not inconsistent with Admiral Tatenen's stated mission of diplomacy."

"But? I heard a tune of *but* there, Spock."

"May I remind the captain that Fleet Admiral Tatenen is traveling under Starfleet Command orders and—"

"And what you did was a violation of regulations, I know. I'll take the responsibility."

"Admiral Kirk, you did not give me orders to scan the nav cube."

"Yes, I did, Mister Spock." He smiled at the tall Vulcan. "How long have we served together, Spock? Are you going to tell me you haven't been paying attention to my subtleties?" He shook his head in mock sadness, then sobered. "This is my ship, Spock; I want to know where we are going."

"Dangerously close to Klingon territory, sir."

"We won't be in violation, however." Kirk shrugged. "Well, let's sit back and enjoy the trip."

Spock nodded absently.

Dinner that evening was quite formal. It was, in fact, one of the most lavish and formal dinners Kirk had ever given. Usually he ate what the men ate, sometimes in his quarters, sometimes with his officers, and on rare occasions and only at their invitation, with the general crew.

Kirk sat at the head of the long table, with Fleet Admiral Tatenen on his right, Baroness Commander Amalia on his left. Tapia, Ogar and Anderson were mixed with the *Enterprise* senior staff: Spock, Uhura, Scott, Sulu, McCoy, Chekov, Leslie, and several others.

There was fresh Khepri *kok-ido* birds, a gift from Tatenen, Altair *zanahoria*, Centauri cavolfiore, Terran potatoes, Axanar *kukurydza*, and Andorian wine-analog. The conversation was brisk and gay, with Tatenen making an attempt to charm Uhura, and succeeding. Kirk noted that the old man's bold charm did not seem to bother Amalia at all, who seemed to ignore it.

Baroness Amalia kept up a conversation with the taciturn Spock, who ate slowly from his vegetarian dish. She spoke of a visit to Vulcan in her early youth with her mother, an ambassador from the Miradi Empire. "She, too, was quite taken with the charm of the Vulcans." Kirk almost choked on his glass of wine. He had never thought of Vulcans as "charming," although they might be many other things. He looked at the baroness but thought she seemed quite sincere. Thinking back, Kirk realized that quite a number of other women had found the austere Spock attractive and a challenge. The smoldering interest of Nurse Chapel, now *Doctor* Chapel, had been almost embarrassingly obvious.

But it was Fleet Admiral Tatenen who dominated the table. With his darkly tanned skin, hawk nose, mane of white hair, and crisp uniform emblazoned with medals, ribbons, and the great Star of Arcturus, he was a most impressive figure.

"Aw, I've told that story a hundred times," he grumbled, responding to Uhura's question about the Battle of Vonra. "Let me tell you about Pakheth, that's right near my home sun of Ra, only three, four light years off." Tatenen launched into an account of a skirmish with Klingon scout ships which was the precursor of the more famous Vonra battle.

Kirk listened, unable to keep from being fascinated. Tatenen told the story with all the flair of a born storyteller, knowing where the thrills and laughs were, disparaging of his own valor, praising others. It was obvious he had told this story, too, many times, but no one minded. To Kirk it was like Nelson telling of the Battle of Trafalgar, or Eisenhower of the Normandy Invasion, or Armstrong of the landing on Earth's moon.

Yet something tugged at Kirk's thoughts. Tatenen seemed to relish in his wholesale destruction of Klingon ships, and in the modestly told accounts of his receptions at Federation headquarters, his great speech at Starfleet Academy, his appearance before the Grand Council. Kirk did not begrudge him the fruits of his victories, nor did he expect doers of great deeds to be unduly modest. It was the *relish* which disturbed him.

After dinner a few were invited to Kirk's quarters, where he talked Federation-Klingon tactics with Tatenen. "You've got to hit them at every opportunity, son. Be aggressive, be bold, attack!"

"But first, surely, you try to avoid war," Kirk said—but Tatenen was not listening.

"The only thing Klingons and Romulans understand is raw power. Strength! Firepower! They are barbarians at the gates of civilization, Kirk! You must hit and hit first!"

"After all other means of diplomacy are exhausted, of course," Spock said.

Tatenen eyed the Vulcan officer with hostile eyes. "No offense, son, 'cause I know you Vulcans are related distantly to the Klingons, and you're not a warlike people, but *they* are. They don't understand about diplomacy. They think that's weakness! You walk down some liberty port—Telemachus, Marsport, old Dronning, Kaksi, any of the Blue Planet ports, Abramsville, any of those. You walk around those streets you're going to get jumped. Or conned. Or sold into slavery, maybe, if you are out near Brin or Prantares. But you walk those streets like you'll *eat* the first one that lays a finger, claw, or tentacle on you and, by the stars, they'll leave you alone!"

Tatenen sat back as if he had said everything there was to say on the subject. Kirk tactfully introduced another subject and the old admiral launched forth on another attack. After a time, Kirk saw Spock quietly and thoughtfully leave.

James Kirk sat in the command chair, watching the stars move, a sight he had never grown tired of. They were so beautiful, he thought, even in the blurred images during warp drive. So colorful, so bright, endlessly appealing.

"Course change," Sulu reported as the stars moved to the left. Kirk nodded. Spock's secret scan had given him the exact course plotted. Pollox IV was not too many hours away. What then, he wondered. Well, you deliver him and go on about your business, that's what you do.

"Captain, there's a ship at extreme sensor range," Lieutenant Nakashima reported.

"Magnify," Kirk ordered. The stars on the forward screen were replaced by a small cluster of dots. "Ships," he said. "Three of them. Uhura, ask for identification." He punched his arm control. "Mister Spock, report to the bridge!"

"They refuse to acknowledge, sir," Uhura said.

"Yellow alert," Kirk ordered and the klaxons sounded. Throughout the ship a yellow band appeared across every screen, and feet hit the deck running. The defensive screens went on.

Spock entered the bridge and strode to his station. Moments later Admiral Tatenen also arrived, along with Captain Tapia and the baroness. "Klingons," the Admiral said, looking at the spectral read-out screen.

"Correct," Spock said. "Three Klingon vessels of the Kl'ar class."

"Uhura, put me through to them."

"Sir, you're on the hailing frequency."

"This is Admiral James T. Kirk of the U.S.S. *Enter-*

prise. You are in Federation territory. Identify yourselves."

There was no answer. Kirk repeated the demand. Nothing. "Are you in difficulty?" Kirk asked, and Admiral Tatenen snorted.

"It's a Klingon trick," he said.

Kirk didn't even look at him. "I must exhaust every option," he said.

"You're losing the advantage," Tatenen said harshly. "They're closing, Kirk. Open fire! They are violating Federation space!"

Kirk's head turned and he stared at the Fleet Admiral. "Sir, with respect, this is my ship."

"Well, you won't *have* a ship if they can get in close enough to concentrate phaser fire from three ships on any one of your screens, Captain Kirk."

Kirk snapped his head back toward the forward screen. "Mister Spock, your assessment?"

"They are in violation of Federation territory, it is true, but hardly enough to start a war over."

"You give them a parsec and they'll take a lightyear, son! I know those Klingons! This is a chance to show them who's boss!"

Kirk looked at the famed officer in surprise. "We are not attempting to decide who is boss, Admiral Tatenen, only to avoid an incident."

"Avoid an incident," mimicked Tatenen acidly. Sulu and Chekov looked around in surprise. Regardless of what they thought of one another, high ranking officers rarely showed animosity in public. Kirk looked stonily impassive. "Turn and run, you mean," Tatenen hissed.

Kirk said to no one in particular, "Clear the bridge of non-essential personnel!" Baroness Amalia gasped and Captain Tapia's hand touched his phaser involuntarily. But Tatenen turned and wordlessly left, followed by his entourage.

"Try again," Kirk told Uhura.

A moment later a smile of relief came over her face. "Captain Kirk, they are Klingon ambassadorial vessels escorting someone called Kaare to Pollox IV."

Kirk looked at Spock. "He must have known," Spock shrugged.

"That's the reason for the trip," Kirk added. He looked slightly sick.

"They are flying under Federation protection," Uhura repeated the message.

Kirk looked at Sulu, who was still poised, his hand ready over the manual override which would have disconnected the ship from the prerecorded control cube and allowed them free movement. "Relax, Mister Sulu. And take the conn. Proceed on course Mister Chekov. Spock . . ."

The two men left the control room and went quickly to Kirk's quarters. Kirk turned and spoke. "What in blazes was he up to? He could have started a war!"

"Exactly, Captain."

Kirk stopped his pacing and looked thoughtfully at his first officer. "His days of glory."

"There are aspects of human psychology which completely elude me, Captain, but I think that would be a logical premise. He desires to provoke some kind of conflict and die in a blaze of glory."

"And not die an old man on a pension," Kirk finished. "Well, we avoided that one."

"Jim, let me remind you—he carries enormous prestige. If we leave after putting him on Pollox IV there will be no one to monitor his actions."

Kirk groaned.

The baroness and the rest of Admiral Tatenen's personal staff stepped up upon the transporter stage, but the white-haired officer hung back a moment and spoke confidentially to Captain Kirk. "Son, let me give you some advice. No, now listen." He thrust a thumb over his shoulder, presumably at the three Klingon ships also in parking orbit. "You keep an eye on those fellas, boy. A sharp eye. The moment you see something out of line, you blast 'em." He held up a hand. "I know, I know, you young officers, well, you don't think that way. But I've been fighting Klingons nigh as long as you've been alive, boy, and bless Ra, I'll go out fighting them—so you listen up. They're tricky, tricky as a yellow *scral* and twice as mean."

He slapped Kirk on the shoulder. "You'll see," he said and gave everyone a big wave as he stepped up on the stage. "Do it to us, boy," he ordered.

Kirk nodded at the Transporter Chief, who pulled down the cycle switch. The party dissolved in beams of sparkling light, and then were gone. Kirk stared at the empty stage thoughtfully, then left the room.

The turbolift door hissed open and Kirk strode onto the bridge. "Admiral on the bridge," Uhura said, getting up from the command chair.

"I have the conn, Commander," Kirk said. "Report."

"We monitored the entertainment frequencies as well as the government ones, Captain Kirk," Uhura said. "All night there were parties and receptions for both the Klingons and Admiral Tatenen. They're not trying to keep it a secret any longer. This afternoon they are supposed to get together to discuss an agenda which has not yet been revealed." She smiled. "But they're calling it the final act in the long Human-Klingon fighting. A new page in history. That sort of thing."

"Hmmm," Kirk muttered, sitting down. "Keep monitoring, Uhura."

The rest of the morning was taken up with administrative duties. Kirk held Captain's Mast, the court for minor violations, taking over the rec room to accommodate the witnesses. An Electrician First was accused of stealing special food from a yeoman with Rigellian bone-stress, and found guilty. Failure to respond quickly enough to alerts got two Specialist Firsts extra duty. A sexual harassment charge against a female nutritionist was dismissed for lack of evidence. A petty officer was accused by Lieutenant Deckert of re-programming one of the computer games to win money from the crew, and found guilty.

Kirk was in his quarters, reviewing a tape of *Tactics in Space War*, by General Sandra Cohen, when Uhura called him. "*Admiral, come to the bridge, please!*"

In moments Kirk was coming through the doors. "Report!" he said.

"Sir, the Klingons have beamed up from the conference. Reporters say they were very angry. Admiral Tatenen has issued a statement that the Klingons were not negotiating in good faith, that it was all a trap, and—"

"Where is he now?" Kirk demanded. He thumbed the general annunciator. "Commander Spock to the bridge!"

Chekov spoke up. "Sir, someone is beaming aboard!"

Kirk's finger hit a button. "Transporter Room, this is Captain Kirk—what's going on there?"

"*Uh, sir, Admiral Tatenen and his party have just—*"

"*Captain Kirk, this is Fleet Admiral Karis Atum Tatenen. I am executing Starfleet Order 1-202-B as of this date and moment. Please log that.*"

Kirk blinked. That was the rarely used regulation which permitted senior officers to commandeer private, commerical, and military spacecraft in emergency situations. Tatenen was taking over the *Enter-*

prise. Spock entered the bridge, eyebrows elevated.

Involuntarily, Kirk's thumb stabbed at a button. "Transporter Room, report! Answer me!"

"Kirk, this is Tatenen, blast you! I am ordering you—"

"Kirk here," he said, his finger punching another button. "Security forces to the transporter room. There's a malfunction of some kind. Contain and report. Kirk out!" He looked at Spock.

"A fascinating situation, Captain," the Vulcan said.

"He did something down there, I know it!" Kirk said. "He deliberately blew the conference. I don't know how, but he did!"

"He gave you a legitimate order," Spock reminded his captain.

Kirk's face assumed an expression of mild surprise. "He did? I didn't hear anything. There's something funny going on down there, Spock. Unauthorized personnel beaming aboard, malfunctioning communications, people hearing things."

"In other words, Captain, if you can delay the admiral long enough the Klingons will have left."

Kirk shrugged. "Why make a bad situation worse? He may have ruined the conference, but at least he won't start a war. Mister Chekov, what is the status of the three Klingon vessels?"

"Shields up, but quiet, sir." He looked around at his captain. "Perhaps they are waiting to see what we do, Keptin."

Kirk nodded. "And we'll do nothing." He saw a movement of Sulu's hand. "No, Mister Sulu! Shields down."

Sulu looked around in surprise. "But, sir, we'll have no protection!"

"I know, Mister Sulu. Uhura, put me through to the Klingon commander."

She nodded and her slim fingers played across the keys. "Klingon commander ready, sir."

"I am Admiral James T. Kirk, of the U.S.S.—"

"KIRK!" The face on the screen was that of Kang, a Klingon captain whom Kirk had met years before. *"Kirk!"* The Klingon's voice was almost friendly. *"We meet again!"*

"Kang!" Kirk said, just as surprised. "I thought they'd . . . discipline you after Beta XII Alpha."

"They did, Kirk, they did, in their way. I'm still a captain and you, you're an admiral." The Klingon, in his dark uniform with the glittering sah, shrugged.

"Is . . . is Mara well?" Kirk asked.

"My wife is well. She retired to care for our daughters."

"Congratulations, Kang!"

"For what, Kirk? They are females!" He all but roared the last word. *"And now your ambassador has put impossible demands upon us!"* Kang appeared monumentally angry. *"My father fought against him at Vonra. He was a brilliant tactician then, but now, now he's a fool! The Klingon Empire cannot possibly consider even one of his preposterous proposals!"*

"You won't have to, Kang, he's—"

"*He threatened us, Kirk, threatened us with you, you and the Enterprise! Well, we are three to one, Kirk. We shall see who journeys to the end of time as a gas, human!*"

"Wait, Kang! There's no need for this!"

"*He insulted us! He belittled us!*"

"Granted, he's no diplomat."

Kang stared at Kirk through the screen and the universal translator. "*No dip . . . lo . . . mat,*" he said slowly, then burst into a torrent of laughter. "*No diplomat!*"

After a moment he sobered and spoke with a calmer manner. "*I have no desire to start a war, Kirk. I attack you, you attack me, one wins, one loses . . . but there will be many deaths. There is no honor in that.*"

"Sounds to me as if you've mellowed, Kang."

Kirk saw a flash of Kang's former anger, then the big, dark Klingon shrugged. "*Maybe . . . even with daughters . . . you think about what is to come.*" Then his eyes bored into Kirk's. "*But if we meet where there is reason to fight, just you and I, ship against ship—!*"

Kirk laughed. "There's the old irrascible Kang we all know and love." Kang glowered some more. "Look, we'll leave together, all right? Then neither is retreating from the other."

"*Done.*" Kang turned at once, his deep voice giving orders.

Kirk spoke, too. "Mister Sulu, warp out of orbit.

Set a course for Regulus III, Warp Five the moment it is safe."

"Aye, sir!"

Kang turned back, something like a smile on his face. *"Kirk, you had best mothball that old admiral. He was first in his day, but . . ."* He shrugged and Kirk nodded.

"Captain!" Uhura said. "Admiral Tatenen has broken out of the transporter room and is going aboard the shuttlecraft *Galileo!*"

"Kang! Don't do anything—" Kirk began.

"I see it," the Klingon snarled, staring at an off-camera screen. *"And I know what he intends to do."* He looked back at Kirk. *"Admiral, I think we are about to do the Federation Starfleet a great service."*

"No—!" But Kang was gone and Kirk fell back into his chair. "Get a tractor beam on them," he ordered. "Get them back aboard!"

"Negative, Captain," Spock said. "He is approaching the Klingons along one of only two routes where we cannot reach him, where the nacelles interfere."

Kirk watched helplessly as the *Galileo* headed straight toward the Klingon vessel at top speed. The Klingon Kl'ar-class ship had its defensive screens up, but they were only effective against radiation, electronic emissions—such as phasers—or fast-moving physical objects, such as bullets. Swift but still slow-moving shuttlecraft could go right through. And Tatenen intended to ram.

"Go to warp speed," muttered Kirk angrily.

"They are too close to each other, Captain," Spock said. "The emissions would pull each other apart."

"Then why don't they—"

A phaser spat a single burst and the shuttlecraft exploded. The bits and pieces which were not vaporized went straight out in a spherical pattern. Eventually they would reach the edge of the galaxy and just keep going.

"Uhura, send this message to Starfleet. 'Fleet Admiral Karis Atum Tatenen, hero of the Battle of Vonra, Destroyer of Klingons, died today on the bridge of a spacecraft after an unfortunate accident. Captain Kang, commander of the Klingon craft which accidently struck Admiral Tatenen's shuttlecraft, expressed deep regret. James T. Kirk, Admiral, U.S.S. Enterprise.' "

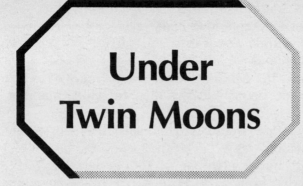

Under Twin Moons

"Liberty port!" Lex Nakashima grinned. The young officer smiled at Lieutenant Commander Uhura and Dr. McCoy sitting in the rec room. Around them off-duty crew members were drinking, snacking, talking, playing cards, and challenging each other to the various complex computer games.

McCoy smiled at the young lieutenant, then looked at Uhura. "I remember some of my early planetfalls, on the *Crockett* and the *Xerxes*," he said, "and what I thought a good liberty port was."

"But it's Macedon III," Nakashima said eagerly, unable to keep the grin off his face.

"And you've heard all about the plume dancers,"

Uhura smiled. "And the New Temple of Zeus, the thieves market, and Queen Daria."

Nakashima nodded. "The Warrior-King, the pool of Circe, and—"

"Hold it!" McCoy laughed, holding up his hand. "Are you being paid by the Macedon Chamber of Commerce?"

"Well, gee, Doctor, this is really *the* liberty port in this sector."

"But not a member of the Federation," Uhura reminded him. "The Empire of Thrace is independent of both the Federation and the Klingon-Romulan Alliance, so don't bring disgrace down on us."

McCoy looked at her in mock surprise. "A sailor on leave bringing trouble . . . ?" They laughed, but Uhura tilted her head at the young officer.

"Remember, Mister Nakashima—deportment . . . but have a good time."

"I think you've just given him a problem he can't solve," McCoy said. Nakashima walked quickly on, waving farewell. "Good man," McCoy said, looking after him. He turned to Uhura. "You going ashore?"

Uhura responded slowly. "No . . . I don't think so, Doctor."

McCoy's manner changed to one of quiet concern. "You should. You didn't go down at Upsilon Xi III nor Lieberman's World. You're going to get cabin fever."

"I'm all right, Doctor, really."

"Young woman, I am the chief medical officer of

this ship and I'm telling you . . . I'm *ordering* you to get some R and R." The beautiful young black woman started to speak but McCoy held up a hand. "That's an order, Commander Uhura. Where matters of health, both physical and psychological, are concerned, I am boss."

Uhura sighed and smiled. "Oh . . . very well . . ."

"The proper response to an order from a superior officer in Starfleet is 'Yes, sir,' " McCoy grinned.

"Yes, sir!"

"And I don't mean to just go planetside and look at the museums. I mean, *have some fun.*"

"Yes, *sir!*" Uhura said, giving him a mock salute. "Fun, sir, yes, sir!"

The shuttlecraft *Columbus* dropped through the atmosphere and arced toward a landing at New Athens. The ship was crowded with happy, chattering officers and men. It was more efficient to take shiploads down in the two shuttlecraft than to beam them down in smaller numbers, but it took longer.

Uhura didn't mind. She looked out at the Class III world curiously. It *had* been a long time since she set foot on the soil of any planet. Or looked up at anything but a ceiling. Or saw further than the length of the rec room. Maybe McCoy was right, she thought. Get out and see something of the galaxy. Stop hiding away in the *Enterprise.*

The heavy cruiser was a big ship, with a great variety of services and entertainments to interest

and amuse the crew, but there were no real surprises. However, a new planet always had surprises.
That was an axiom of space travel.

Macedon had been populated early in the days of
human space exploration by an ethnic group from
Earth, arriving via sleeper ships. They had mixed
easily with the native humanoids, remnants of a
war-devasted race called the Thracians. All this had
occurred well before the strong enforcement of the
Federation's Prime Directive, that rule of noninterference with the normal development of alien life
and societies.

Despite her initial disinclination, Uhura felt the
fast pulse of excitement creep over her. There was
nothing to fear, she thought. Thrace and the Federation were on excellent terms, even if Thrace was also
on good terms with the Klingons. Nothing to fear,
that is, except what one might fear in any liberty
port from San Francisco to Marsport or Telemachus
on Tellar. Thieves, con-men, drunks, dippers, people
with a hatred for the Federation—these were the
standard dangers.

No, she thought, I've nothing unusual to fear.
Then why am I getting nervous? she thought.

New Athens was not a large city. The Thracians
had believed in small cities, 25,000 to 50,000 at
most, where it was possible that everyone might
know everyone else, or at least know them by sight
or reputation. The buildings were not large, and
despite the names transplanted from Terra, they

were not in the classical Greek architectural style,
but did have a certain faint functional resemblance.
The weather was usually warm, so therefore they
built structures with deep columned porches to cap-
ture and cool the wind, and the building material
was mostly smoothly shaped stone.

But the ornamentation was totally abstract, some-
what like the geometrical designs of Arabia. Even the
statues were non-representational, based more on
the "auras" of each people "sculpted" than upon
their physical appearance. Flowering trees called the
ormachi were everywhere, with dark green leaves
and scores of red, yellow, and orange flowers. As a
result there were many insects, but they had a kind
of radar which kept them from hitting or landing on
any living thing. It took Uhura some time to stop
ducking and waving at the fat bugs, but when none
touched her she soon adjusted. Once the double
suns had gone below the horizon the evenings were
nearly totally free of any insects.

Uhura stood on the wide terrace of Hotel Terra,
where Federation personnel usually stayed. The hotel was on a hill and she could see the other hills of
New Athens, and on the highest hill, the New Temple of Zeus. The palace of the Warrior-King was
further away, a stark fortress of black stone topped
by crimson-capped towers. A bird, glutted with his
daily gorging of insects, flopped lazily by. There was
music from the ballroom and the scent of the night-
blooming Moonflowers.

And, of course, the two moons, Circe and Artemis,

casting pale double shadows across the terrace. Uhura sighed. It *was* good to put her feet on something besides a deck, to breathe scents instead of filtered, tasteless air.

I missed it, she thought. I miss him, too, she sighed. It had been a long time, a very long time. Jomo Murumbi, Captain, Special Forces, United States of Africa, killed in the performance of his duties, 16 October 2164, Obbia, Somalia. R.I.P.

Uhura looked at the moons. All right, she told herself, get yourself out of it. It's been long enough, girl! You were not a widow, yet you've acted like one most of the time!

Get on with your life!

"Good evening."

Uhura turned at the sound of a deep voice and saw a handsome man smiling at her. Surprised, she could only say, "Uh, good evening." But her thoughts were different: *Great Stars, he's attractive!* This was followed in a microsecond by her next thought: A man this attractive is either married or a rat.

"I hope you don't mind," he said. "I couldn't help speaking to you. I saw you inside and . . ." He hesitated, then smiled. "I am violating some sort of protocol, I'm sure, but I had to speak to you."

"That's all right," she said quickly, perhaps too quickly. She turned to the terrace railing and looked out at the moonlit city. "I was just admiring the view."

"It is nice, isn't it?" he said, stepping to her side.

Careful, girl, she told herself, your breathing is giving you away. "That's the palace, right? And the Temple of Zeus?"

"The *New* Temple of Zeus," he corrected. "That," he pointed, "is the Museum of Terran History. Next to it, the Museum of the History of Thrace. See that dome? That's the tomb of Alexander, the first king of the Empire of Thrace."

Uhura smiled. "Sounds very . . . Grecian . . ."

The man smiled. "He was just a touch presumptive, I think. He was born Murray Fox in some suburb of Greater New York, but like many powerful leaders—Hitler, Stalin, the popes, Caligula, Zog, Philistra—he changed his name to something more suitable."

"Like an actor."

"Like an actor," he agreed. "Recasting himself in the mold he found himself in. And you? What do they call you?"

"Uhura. Nyota Uhura." She raised her eyebrows and he responded.

"Jaral." He took her hand and kissed it, bowing slightly. "How may I be of service to a commander of the Federation forces?"

She tilted her head. "By telling me what brings you here, to the tourist trap."

He smiled. He was dark-skinned, dark-eyed, his hand—still holding hers—was strong and warm. "Duty, Commander. I escorted the Matriarch to meet your Captain Kirk." He looked back across the terrace, where, through the high narrow windows they could see the dancers and the clot of uniforms around someone unseen.

"But why aren't you at her side?" Uhura smiled.

"I saw you." He waved across the ballroom. "Besides, my aunt is quite capable of caring for herself. I am only window dressing."

Uhura let her gaze wander over his tall, broad-shouldered figure, taking in the ornate breastplate with the stylized Gorgon head, the epaulets with insignia she did not recognize, and the wrist communicator of the latest Terran design. "It must be a pretty fancy window," she murmured, then regretted her comment.

He shrugged. "I'm afraid I'm so used to dressing a certain way I forgot what it is like to have options."

Uhura nodded. "Me, too. I've worn a uniform so long, I think I'd be confused if I had to decide. They are already talking about a *new* uniform for Starfleet. You've been in . . . in the service long?"

"All my life," he said, moving distressingly close. "I was born a hereditary colonel. I wore a little colonel's suit when I was five," he laughed. "I kept stumbling over the sword."

"Hereditary colonel," Uhura said. "Might there be some indication of rank to go with that?" she asked, indicating his breastplate and insignia.

He looked at her a moment. "I hesitate because . . . well, too often it comes between people."

Uhura smiled. "What are you, Jaral? Head of the Secret Police? Head of the Assassin's Guild?" She found herself wanting to know. This was the first man who had stirred her at all in a very long time.

He bowed again, "Commander Uhura, allow me to present myself. Jaral Perseus Anakreon Jasteel Demetrius Stephanopoulos, Hereditary Colonel of the Companions of Alexander, Count of Samos, Baron of Bactria, Prince Jaral of Sparta, Order of the Shield of Medusa, Star of Apollo, Protector of Delphi, and Sworn Warrior of the Empire of Thrace."

Uhura just stared at him. "You may call me Jaral," he smiled. He peered at her. "See? What did I say? An accident of birth and it keeps everyone away. Look at me, the poor prince, alone in my black stone castle at Samos with no one to play with, desperate for friendship, rejected by—"

Uhura's sudden laughter caused him to stop. They smiled at each other. "I'm just here on leave," she said softly. A touch of fear crept into her mind. He was like Jomo, yet not. This one was far more sophisticated and, therefore, in her mind, more dangerous.

"Then we must take advantage of every moment," he said. He looked toward the ballroom. "Come on, I've got to get the old vulture an escort home."

"But—" He grabbed her hand and they hurried across the smooth stone terrace into the hustle and bustle of a fancy dress ball. There were Thracian men and women, tall, graceful, and pale, in togalike garments of many soft hues. There were the descendants of the Terran settlers in uniforms, formal civilian wear, and togas. Uhura spotted Captain Kirk, in his full fancy uniform as an Admiral in the Starfleet of the United Federation of Planets, with every medal on display and a wide smile on his face. There were others around: Mister Spock in full uniform, spotless and perfect; a slightly rumpled Commander Scott; McCoy with a Thracian beauty on either side; Sulu; Chekov; and Leslie, the A-and-A officer.

But it was the women to whom Kirk was talking that seized her attention. This "old vulture" was a beautiful woman in her early fifties, pale skin unlined, dressed in a simple dark gown with fire rubies, and opals, and a headdress of gold filigree, pinpearls, and delicate orix shells. She laughed at something Kirk had said, then saw Jaral. Her smiling eyes went to Uhura and in that moment Uhura knew she had been analyzed, filed, and classified. "Jaral," she said, "who is this lovely creature?"

"Matriarch, this is Lieutenant Commander Nyota Uhura, of the U.S.S. *Enterprise*. Commander, this is Miranie of Sparta, Priestess of Artemis, Duchess of Korai, Keeper of the Sacred Flame, Matriarch of New Athens—and my aunt."

Uhura unaccountably found a smile tugging at her lips. She bowed very slightly. As a free citizen of the United States of Africa and as a member of the Federation, she thought herself equal to anyone in a certain sense. She would bow, and bow deeply, to any Japanese, for that was a cultural thing like shaking hands, but to bow in deference was something else again.

A very slight narrowing of the eyes betrayed the Matriarch's acknowledgement of Uhura's unspoken comment. "Are you enjoying yourself, Commander?" the older woman said, smiling.

"It is a lovely city," Uhura said, well aware that everyone was listening. Well, she thought, you can't have a conversation with someone like the Matriarch and not have everyone listen in.

"Tomorrow I am showing the commander the pool of Circe, the Fireflower Islands, and perhaps the Sea of Argos," Jaral added. Uhura looked at him curiously. He had lied with such a calm certainty that he must be practiced, she thought.

"Be careful of my nephew, Commander," the Matriarch said. "He is the premier breaker of hearts on this continent."

"Why, Matriarch, you do me an injustice," Jaral said. "You forget I visit Apollonia and Byzantion every year." Before she could say anything Jaral turned to Kirk. "Admiral, with your permission, I should like to show the wonders of New Athens to your lovely commander this night."

Kirk looked at Uhura and raised his eyebrows. Her eyes dropped. "Very well, Prince Jaral, but remember, my officers must be back aboard within forty-six hours."

Uhura shot her captain a dark look. But she had trapped herself by not protesting when Jaral had announced their travel plans. But Captain Kirk, she thought, should not presume so much.

"Admiral," Jaral said. "I wonder if you might escort the Matriarch home?" Kirk bowed a pleased consent. "With your permission, Auntie," Jaral said with a smile.

She sniffed at the "auntie," but waved him away and turned with a bright smile to Spock. "I am fascinated by Vulcans," she said. "They seem so much different than us."

"That is because we are, milady," Spock said.

Jaral pulled Uhura through the throng of people surrounding the Matriarch and Kirk, but at the edge of the crowd Uhura stopped. "Don't you think you could have asked me?"she demanded.

He turned a charming smile on her. "But you do want to see all those things, don't you? Everyone does, even we of Thrace."

"Yes, but—"

"Then let us set forth for the first of them. The ruins of Corin by moonlight." He took her elbow and guided her along to an exit. "Some say it is the greatest romantic sight in the galaxy . . . but I'm certain they must be Thracians who say that."

Despite herself, Uhura was intrigued. This handsome, perhaps overly confident man was determined to sweep her off her feet. It was an exhilarating feeling. "Corin," she said. "Isn't that the ruin of the great temple, from before Terrans came?"

"Yes," he said, returning the salute of the guards at the hotel exit. A lifted hand brought them a carriage, drawn by four deerlike creatures with bells on their harnesses. "To Corin," he ordered the driver, an elderly Thracian.

They went down the hotel hill and across a park, up narrow streets between old buildings, then into another populated valley. But as they started up another hill the houses gave way to tombs, and then ruins of old structures in a very different style of architecture. The columns were shorter and thicker, bulging in the center, with ornate capitals. The windows in the ruined walls were round, the buildings smaller.

"Corin was the palace of the Farkash dynasty," Jaral said. "They were long gone and the Thracians had been thrust back to hunters and hunter-gatherers by the time my ancestors came. War, plague, ego." He shrugged. "An old story. The other race, the Thracians, were wiped out. We rebuilt, incorporating the remaining Thracians into government and society."

"Instead of a slave race, as some might have," Uhura said.

Jaral nodded. The carriage came to the top of the hill. They could see the lights of New Athens, but it was the ruins which attracted the attention of the Federation officer.

They were immense: crumbling carved walls, thick and forbidding. Scenes of war and triumph were still to be seen, muted by time and weather. Ancient humanoid kings on lavish thrones, surrounded by proud generals, with captured princes at their feet and naked slaves bearing treasure were a repeated theme.

They got out and strolled amid the falling stones. Here was a nicked chopping block of granite used by executioners, there the feet and legs of a broken statue to a forgotten Warrior-King. The roofs had all fallen in, but the notches and openings for the great beams of *cari* wood could be seen, usually filled with bird nests. A turning of a wall had sheltered a mural of glazed brick, and in the twin moonlight Uhura could make out a scene of harvest, with slaves and a harvest goddess looming over a sacrificial victim.

She shivered. "They were bloodthirsty."

"No more than our own ancestors," Jaral said. He gestured around him. "This is a reminder of what happens to civilizations who build on cruelty and slavery, who live by aggression and war."

They walked on, on paths of crushed stone bordered by weeds. Here and there gleamed a night-flower like a stationary firefly, sending out its tiny beacon to the only insect who flew the night, the darkbeetle.

There was a rustle behind them and footsteps. Surprised, Jaral turned, his hand going toward his sword, but the dark figures were upon them, truncheons raised. Uhura cried out in surprise, then grabbed the wrist of one attacker and flipped him into a pile of stones. A club struck at her, hitting her left shoulder and numbing it to the elbow. Jaral grunted as two of them struck at him. He staggered, slashing out with his sword, making one of the attackers scream and bend over. Jaral raised his weapon for another strike but someone threw a club and hit him across the throat. He choked and fell, and the sword was knocked from his hand.

Uhura kicked out and felled one attacker, but there were too many of them. Something made a great white light in her head and she was blinded, falling forward into darkness.

A kick in her side aroused her. She groaned and made herself open her eyes. Her head throbbed viciously and her side, thigh, and shoulder were stiff and badly bruised.

She was in some kind of stone room. Her uniform jacket had been removed and her wrists were tied. She shifted her sore body to look up at whoever had kicked her and saw a dark, raggedy man looming over her. "Who the blazes are you?" she demanded. "I'm a Federation officer and—"

She cried out as he kicked her viciously in the side. She rolled away from him, wincing at the fragments of stone which struck into her. Then she saw Prince Jaral. He was unconscious, his head still oozing blood. His hands were tied and his breast-plate and most of the uniform had been taken away, leaving him in tight trousers and a thin, collarless shirt.

Their captor pointed at a wooden bucket of water and some pads of bandages which looked none too clean. "Take care o' him," he grunted.

"Who are you?" Uhura demanded, getting to her knees painfully. "Why did you—" She broke off to avoid another kick.

"Fix 'im," the man said and left, slamming the thick wooden door behind him.

Uhura dragged over the bucket and rinsed off his head wound as best she could with her tied wrists. Then she awkwardly bandaged his head and sat back to wait. She tried to use her teeth on her bonds but the knots were underneath and she couldn't get to them very well.

After about an hour Jaral groaned and opened his eyes. Uhura was at his side at once, inquiring about his head. "I'm . . . I'm all right," he said, "for a man who's lost half his scalp."

Uhura held up her bound wrists. "Do something." With his stiff, bloody fingers Jaral untied her bonds after several tries. Then she untied his. "Not that this is going to do much good," she said, gesturing at the thick door. "Who are these ambushers?"

"Oh, the Traasmeen. They're revolutionists."

Uhura looked at him a moment. "Does the Kingdom of Thrace need a revolution? What are you doing, or not doing, that gets your citizens upset?"

Jaral sat up and shrugged, wincing as he held his head. "There are always malcontents."

"Uh-huh," Uhura said. "That's probably what they called George Washington and the Continental Congress . . . or the men who stormed the Bastille or the Winter Palace."

"They are Turks, in a manner of speaking. They

have intermarried with the original Thracians and . . . well, there are some ancient hatreds which die very slowly."

"Are *we* going to die very slowly, by the way?" she asked.

Jaral nodded, still feeling his head. "Yes, I imagine so. I'm afraid I misjudged them. It was my regiment which defeated them in Byzantion three months ago. I wasn't even there, but . . ." He shrugged and winced. "So they will make my execution very . . . public." He looked up at her, pain in his eyes. "Please forgive me. I got you into this, but I had no idea they had a cell here. There are not many, but . . . they are good at the 'surgical' strike. To remove a prince in the capital city, to make him an example . . ." He made a slight gesture. "It is what I'd do, in their position."

"And what will you do in *your* position?"

He managed a weak smile. "Either one of two things—either escape or try to manage a dignified death."

"Would you mind working first on escaping?" she said. "They took my communicator, or we could just beam up to the *Enterprise*. And they don't expect me back for two days."

"We'll be dead by then. They'll thumb their noses at the Federation, too, with your death. They are fanatics, terrorists."

"Why don't you just give them some place to live?"

"Because they will not take the offer. They are

perhaps four percent of the population, but they want to govern. No one else wants them to govern, especially not those of Greek descent. It would be a bloodbath. We have tried to talk reason, but they break treaties, change their demands, kill our ambassadors. They think to terrorize us into slavery." He shrugged. "That, of course, will never happen. They are most unrealistic. Political amateurs with huge egos. We would try to live in peace with them, but . . ." He shrugged and winced in pain. He managed a smile, though it obviously hurt. "There is only one consolation in all this."

"Great stars, *what*?" Uhura said in surprise.

"To have my last sight be you."

She stared at him a moment, and then her shoulders slumped. "Oh, great. Beautiful. We are about to get sacrificed for some cause I never heard of and *you* get romantic." Her eyes rolled toward the ceiling. He looked embarrassed.

"But it is *true!*" he protested. He reached for her but she got up and moved away. "Nyota!"

Uhura turned back to look at him. "You know, maybe these people *do* have a point in what they're doing if the leaders here are all like you. Oh, you're charming. You're handsome. You're a prince. Me, with a *prince!* You look and sound and act like all the handsome dashing princes a girl ever reads about . . . except for one thing."

"And that is?" he said a bit stiffly.

"That we're about to become sacrificial victims in

some political struggle of which I know almost *nothing!*" She leaned toward him. "And what are you doing about it?"

He touched his head. "Uh . . . thinking of a way to escape."

Uhura crossed her arms and looked at him. After a moment of embarrassed silence he spread his hands. "I can't think with you looking at me like that!"

She snorted as she turned away, impatiently looking around the small stone cell. "We . . . we could overpower the guard," he suggested.

"With what?" she asked. "You have a bashed-in head and they have weapons."

"We're not tied up anymore," he said. "We could *pretend* to still be tied . . ."

"And?"

"And, uh, jump them. That's it."

Uhura made a face. "I've seen this one before. You . . . no, *I*, pretend to be sick. I moan and groan and you shout for the guard and he rushes in and you sock him and we grab his weapon and shoot our way out."

He smiled. "You pick things up quickly."

Uhura gave a most unladylike snort. "Oh, come on, grow up! Half the movies in history wouldn't have gotten past the second reel without dumb guards. But that's in *fiction.*"

"Well, uh, maybe they wouldn't be, you know, guards if they were very smart to begin with. After all, advancement can't be very much. They associate with the lowest kind. Prisons definitely smell . . ." He looked around. "Can't do you much good aesthetically around places like this, either."

"Those are prison guards, Prince. These are revolutionists. There *must* be a difference."

"Umm," Prince Jaral said thoughtfully. "Can't think what it might be. Pay's no good in these revolutionary armies, if you ever get paid at all. I suppose there's something in loot. Possibly pillage, too. Or is pillage the process of obtaining loot? A certain amount of freedom of choice, I imagine. But then, most prison guards have a lifetime job with a pension." He looked at Uhura. "No, can't imagine what the difference might be."

She gave him a long look. "You really *were* hit on the head, weren't you?" She went over and sat beside him on the cot. "Look, Prince—Jaral—we've got to work together. It'll take everything we have to overcome all this."

He smiled at her. "Any suggestions?"

She sighed. "Yes . . uh . . . look, I hope you won't take this too badly, but . . . well, you *were* the one badly hurt, so it would be more natural if *you* were the one to try the dying trick."

"Oh! You really want to try my suggestion of luring the guards?" She nodded. "Oh, good, I thought it might be too, um, unconventional."

Uhura looked at him a moment. "Macedon really *is* a long way out, isn't it?" She sighed again. "All right, look. You lie there looking close to death, but in a position to grab him if he comes close."

"Like this?" he said and stretched out dramatically.

"Uh, no, try this," she said, putting his feet together and straightening him on the cot. "Do you think you could, ah, try to bleed a little?"

He blinked at her. "I didn't think I'd stopped, the way it hurts and all."

"You know, Prince, you are one guy on the ballroom floor and a different one here."

He smiled weakly. "So are you, Lieutenant Commander Uhura. So soft and lovely on the terrace, such a chained tiger here."

Uhura managed a smile. "You know, I think you're right. Now get your act going. Groans, I want groans."

He began to groan, and as he got more into it, he modified into a few moans as well. Uhura ran to the door and pounded on it. "He's dying, you scabrous marshcats! Help him! He's Prince Jaral—you can't just let him *die!* Not like this! Help! Listen, you—"

The door rattled open and Uhura was looking into the muzzle of a weapon she did not recognize, but she recognized the steady hand and the impassive face. "Back up," he growled. She backed up. His eyes slide across to Jaral. "So he's sick, so what?"

"Not sick, dying!" she said loudly. "He's had a hemorhage! He's going to *die,* can't you see that? What good is it if he dies *here,* you idiot?"

His impassive face and dead eyes swung around to look at Uhura. "What's it to you? Think you'd want to see our plans fail."

"Uh . . ." For a moment she had no answer, but then she thought something like the truth might help. "Because the longer he's alive, I'm alive and as long as I'm alive there's a chance to get out of this."

Their captor made a rude sound and his eyes crinkled in what could have been an unborn smile. "Not likely," he said. "What does he need then?"

"How do I know, I'm not a doctor! Look at him yourself. In your line of work you must have seen a few bashes."

He nodded and walked over, as lithe as a cat, his big strange weapon in his fist. Jaral let out a groan and started to thrash around a bit. "Ohhh," he groaned. "No . . . I don't want to die . . . no . . . Mother . . . Matriarch! No, I'm . . . uh . . . *ohhh* . . ."

The thug bent over Jaral but the gun was right in his stomach. "Lemme see that, princey. Aw, blazes, that's not bad. You aristocrats are all alike, thin-blooded."

Jaral opened his eyes. "Mother . . . Mother, you've come . . . I couldn't die without . . . without seeing you . . . kiss me Mother, kiss me!" Jaral reached up and put his arms around the thug's neck and pulled him down. The thug's eyes bulged and he cried out.

"Hey! Watcha doin', you—"

The gun was away from Jaral's stomach and Uhura leaped into the air and kicked with both feet against the side of the jailer's head. He fell with a clatter and lay still.

Jaral rolled from the bed and grabbed the weapon. He groaned and staggered, but led the way toward

the cell door. There were two more of the revolution-
aries in the outer room, but neither of them moved
fast enough.

They were on the streets in moments. "It's the
garit-crafter's street," he said. "This way!"

"I'll relieve you, Liz," Uhura said to Elizabeth
Palmer, who got up, stretched, and left the bridge.
Captain Kirk swiveled his chair around and smiled
at her. On the main screen Macedon was dwindling
fast.

"Did you enjoy liberty?" he asked.

She pursed her lips and thought a moment. "Yes,
Captain. Macedon was very . . . educational."

Kirk's smile widened. "Who learned from whom,
Commander?"

"Why, Captain Kirk," she said. "You know the
Federation policy. To render aid and assistance at
every opportunity."

"I thought as much," Kirk said and swiveled toward the screen. "Warp Four, Mister Sulu."

"Aye, sir."

Wild Card

The savannah spread out from the knoll in every direction, a vast shallow lake of marshes and tiny islands, of lush green plants and tall, tan grasses. Lieutenant Commander Hikaru Sulu stood on the knoll and breathed in the pungent air with a smile.

Insects whizzed and buzzed and fluttered by. From time to time one landed on his yellow protection suit and for the most part he either studied or ignored them. Once in a while something the size of his hand landed with a sticky plop and started to gnaw away at the tough levfrum material. Then he pried it off with a stick and went back to enjoying the ecological splendor of Marris V, under the bright yellow sun of its primary star and the distant orange dwarf of its secondary.

Sulu almost didn't know where to start collecting. To his right were clusters of tall vanelike plants of a reddish color, wreathed in strings of sticky ooze in which insects were trapped. At night the vanes rolled shut and the digestive processes began. Behind him were some large white, yellow-tinged flowers that smelled of both chocolate and turpentine. On his left were low, wide-leafed plants bearing small dark-blue berries which his tricorder said were mostly strychnine and lacrose.

Ahead of him, at the edge of the grassy mound which only rose a few feet above the marshy surface, was a nest of some kind, a long hutlike structure made of leaves, grass, and twigs. He walked over and looked inside. It was dark, but something scurried about.

"Mister Sulu, report in, please."

Sulu pulled his communicator from the zippered pocket in his protection suit and flipped it open. "Sulu here, Uhura. What's up?"

"Better hurry back, Hikaru. We have only two hours until we sail on."

Sulu sighed. There was so much to see and collect and report on. He felt like Darwin in the Galapagos, Alfred Russel Wallace in South America, Charles Lee Jackson on Rigel III. Everything new and exciting, wonderful, and mysterious.

"An hour, Uhura, just an hour."

"All right, but I warned you. Admiral Kirk has finished the duty call on the manager at Automate-66 and is coming back aboard."

"Understand. Sulu out." He tucked away the communicator as he looked over the marsh critter's nest. There was only one Federation presence on Marris V, the pylene plant on the other side of the planet. The clod there, he had noted, wasn't the least interested in botany, zoology, parallel evolution, biochemistry, ethnology, entomology, or any of the things the young Oriental officer thought important. That was all right, not being interested, for after all, one cannot be really interested in *everything*, but to be offered the chance to study an entire planet and to refuse was, to his mind, almost criminal.

On Marris V an ecology had been achieved and had functioned for millions of years without raising, as far as they could tell, a single intelligent life form. That in itself was not unique: there were millions of Earth-like planets in the Milky Way galaxy and only a relatively few had produced intelligences equal to man's. But the ecology was a vast one, for it was nearly the same throughout the entire marshy surface of the world. *That* was unique and Sulu wanted to know why.

But then, he smiled to himself, I always want to know *why*. He caught an orange bug with brown wings and put it in his collection box and pressed the stunning button. Then he bent over and looked into the nest again. He caught the glint of eyes and drew back, pulling his phaser. He checked it to see if it was still set on Stun, then started to crawl into the nest.

The whole nest swayed a bit and he heard ripping noises, so he backed out quickly. He examined the nest and realized it was floating on the water, tied to the plants at the edge of the shore. He didn't want to do any more damage, so he stood up and moved along the shore, inspecting the nest and making a 3-D record with a camera.

Then he saw a movement, a rippling of the water away from the nest. He aimed and fired his phaser and the movement ceased. A blob of green floated to the surface and Sulu walked carefully into the water and scooped it up in a naturalist's fine-webbed net. It was just a gobbet of greenery, the roots to some plant.

"It must have gotten away," he muttered.

"Mister Sulu, this is the Enterprise. *Report, please."*

Sulu made a face, waded back to the relatively dry shore and plopped the root system into his collection box. He plucked out his communicator and spoke rather testily. "Sulu here. What is it?"

"Move it, Sulu," Uhura said. *"Captain wants out sooner. You're almost the last one."*

"All right, all right. Wait until I decon." He unzipped his decontamination tube from a waterproof pocket and sprayed it all over himself and the imperv-plastic collection box. The hard ultraviolet rays would rupture the cell walls of almost any sort of plant life and the other ray emitting from the tube would sterilize almost any bacteria known. He would be beamed directly to the decon transporter room and be bathed in even stronger decontamination rays, walk through a decon bath and take another UV "shower." He put the decon tube away and spoke into his communicator. "Mister Leslie, beam me up."

For a moment he was a column of dazzling, sparkling light. Then he was gone. There was nothing on the knoll. A bird flopped across the sky. Something splashed out in the lake. In the nest was heard a small series of faint, plaintive sounds.

Lex Nakashima and Sulu bent over the microscope, adjusting a specimen slice. "There," Sulu said, looking at the large, 5,000-line screen. "Interesting, but nothing extraordinary."

"Chalk up another one for parallel evolution in similar environments," Lex said. He bent over and looked at the insects Sulu had brought back. They had been dried and needed only to be mounted into Sulu's growing display of xenobiological specimens.

Sulu looked at his chronometer. "Uh-oh, gotta run. I have a lecture to give the assistant navigators in ten minutes. Uh . . ."

Lex smiled. "I'll clean up, don't worry. You want these bugs with standard mountings?"

"Yeah, fine, I appreciate it." He paused to sign the small form attesting that he had followed Standard Decontamination Procedures in securing the specimen, then shoved it toward Lex. "Sign that when you get a chance, will you? Look, I gotta go."

"Then go." He waved Sulu off and turned his gaze to the screen again. Briefly, he wondered if the transporter's molecular reassemble could possibly affect a specimen. Starfleet stoutly maintained the replicant was identical, but the *Enterprise* had had trouble during ion storms, and at other times.

He shrugged and boxed the slide, then turned his attention to the strange little bugs Sulu had brought back. They had been killed with the adapted phaser stunning technique, then bathed several times with the ultraviolet. Quite safe, he thought. He picked one up with tweezers and prepared to mount it. He stared with sudden curiosity at the chitinous body covering of the insect. It was different from anything he had seen before, almost metallic. And it covered almost all of the sensitive body torso.

"You really have a pretty good armor there, li'l buggie." He put it under a waldoed magnifier and saw a fine dust filter from the edges of the carapace, but thought nothing much about it. It had come from a swampy planet; the insect was certain to have a water film of some sort; time, decon, and UV had dried the film and the dust was the dead effluvium left after the water had evaporated.

"All right," Nakashima said, "now for your moment of glory—eternal rest in the collection of Lieutenant Commander Hikaru Sulu." Deftly, Lex mounted the bug, then turned to the next.

He sneezed and almost dropped the third specimen. Too bad Sulu didn't have two of that first bug, he thought. I'd have loved to run that chitin through the analyzer. His nose began to itch, and then there was a sudden stab of pain.

He touched his finger to his nose and took it away with blood on it. He blinked in surprise, as he rarely got nosebleeds. Then the headache started. He tried to ignore it for several seconds, but it just kept getting worse. He dropped his tweezers and clutched the edge of the table in sudden pain. He cried out, inhaled, and screamed.

Sulu pressed his hand against the wall plate and his cabin door hissed open. "Oh, hi, Lex," he said to Nakashima. "Sorry I had to run. You put everything away okay?"

Nakashima nodded slowly. His eyes were wet and he seemed flushed, but Sulu didn't notice. He was washing up in the sonic shower. "Hey, Lex!" he called. Lex looked toward the bathroom. "Lex? What do you think of that midshipman we took aboard at Axanar, huh? Linda Chang? Isn't she something, though?"

Sulu came out pulling on a fresh uniform. "Oh, that feels good. Did you hear me about—hey, you okay? You look, uh, kind of strange." He put a hand to Nakashima's forehead. "Hey! You're feverish! I'd better get—"

"No," Nakashima said and put his hand across face. Sulu yelled—then screamed.

"Midshipman Chang? I'm Lieutenant Commander Sulu."

"Yes, sir, I know who you are," she smiled. She looked at Lieutenant Sulu and smiled politely.

"I wonder if you'd mind coming down to the lab. I was looking through our dossier and I noticed something I think you could help us with. You have a degree from the University of South Wales in botany."

"Yes, sir. They have a fine xenobiology lab there."

"Exactly. It's right down this way. We ran across something on Marris V that we can't quite classify."

"Of course," she said, smiling at the handsome officer. She knew who Commander Sulu was all right. There weren't that many of the "old" *Enterprise* crew on board, and everyone knew who they were.

They entered the lab and Linda said, "Where is the—" She jumped as Nakashima put his hand across her face. She felt like acid was striking at her and she screamed, then filled her lungs to scream again.

"Oh, Lieutenant Langhorne? It's me, Linda Chang."

His cabin door hissed open, and she smiled wanly and said, "May I come in? Are you alone?"

"Sure," he said, his smile widening.

Scott looked up at the interruption, then glanced at his chronometer. There was no real night and day on a starship, but the human rhythms still required it. An artificial night was in effect. Most of the crew were off duty. He put down the control with which he had been scanning *Warp Stresses in Real Time* and pressed a communicator stud. "Who is it?"

"Sulu, Scotty."

"Ah, lad, good of you . . ." Scotty opened the door to his cabin and Sulu entered at his gesture. "A wee drop, lad? I have some fine Triacus pod wine, and there's a bit of that Rigellian *dorf* left."

"No, thank you," Sulu said and put his hand out. Without thinking, Scotty took the offered hand. "What are ye congratulating me about, lad, I—" His eyes bulged and the muscles of his neck grew taut. Sulu seized his wrist and held the hand of the powerful officer tightly.

Scott's yell of pain became a shriek of agony.

McCoy smiled as he lifted the pressure-hypo from the arm of Captain Kirk. "There you are, Jim, the perfect answer to the little weight problem."

Kirk gave him a glum look. "Changing my body chemistry so that I can't assimilate right-handed sugars seems like medieval alchemy, Bones."

"Perfectly respectable therapy, Jim. Davis completed a ten-year study. Read about it in the *New England Journal of Medicine*. The human body evolved utilizing right-handed sugars; essentially it's blind to left-handed sugars—"

"Left-hand, right-hand, what does that mean?"

"It means that when you send polarized light through a crystaline structure one kind sends the light to the right, the other kind through the left. You can eat all you want, you won't feel hungry, but for about twenty-seven hours nothing will take."

"I'll starve!"

"You won't starve. You'll have bulk, your hunger center will be flim-flammed, and you'll lose extra pounds."

"Ounces."

"Exercise, too, of course."

"Magic, that's what it is." Kirk picked up the bottle from which McCoy had loaded the syringe. "Eye of bat and toe of dog, wool of bat and blind worm's sting. Very hygienic."

"Go. Go be a starship boss. Leave me to people who are really sick."

"Who's sick?"

"Nobody, but I have a lot of reading to catch up on."

Kirk smiled and left the sickbay. He saw Nakashima and Sulu ahead in the corridor and smiled at them. "What's wrong?" he asked. "You two look as if you've just lost an election bet."

"Admiral Kirk," Sulu said. "I wonder if you could go with us to Lab 12?"

"Why? What's up?"

"Something I found on Marris V, sir. Can't figure it out."

"You want Doctor McCoy, not me. He's back there now. Tell him I'm sorry about his reading." Kirk started to step around Sulu, but the young officer grabbed his hand tightly.

Kirk stopped. He felt a tingling and thought: The antistatic flooring isn't working. "What is it, Sulu?"

"Uh, nothing, sir." Sulu looked confused. He dropped Kirk's hand. "I . . . I thought you were . . ."

"Falling," said Nakashima. "He thought you were falling."

Kirk smiled. "Gentlemen, what you do on your own time is your business, as long as it doesn't interfere with the running of the ship. But . . ." He leaned closer and spoke in a whisper. "I wouldn't call on Engineer Scott so often."

Briskly, he turned and strode away down the corridor. Sulu looked at Nakashima, amazement in his eyes.

Captain James T. Kirk came onto the bridge and motioned down Lieutenant Commander Uhura, who had the conn. She sat back in the captain's chair and stared straight ahead at the main screen.

"Everything all right, Uhura?" he asked.

"Everything is all right, Admiral," Uhura answered.

"What's our ETA at Omicron Theta, Mister Sulu?"

"Fourteen hours, forty-one minutes, sir."

Kirk frowned. "That soon?" He shrugged, thinking he must have lost track of things for a moment. His rough estimate had been eight or nine hours longer. "Very well, carry on."

Kirk left the bridge. No one spoke. Lieutenant Commander Sulu punched up another set of coordinates. Read-out screens showed a different set of numbers, but no one said anything.

"It's me, Spock," Kirk said into the door announcer. The doors hissed open and he entered. To his left Spock sat in a black robe, meditating in a niche. Very slowly Spock came back to his present surroundings and looked at his captain.

"Yes, Admiral?"

Kirk waved his hand and took a comfortable seat. "Don't Admiral me, Spock. I need your advice."

"Of course . . . Jim." Spock rose and stood ready, his concentration on Kirk quite intense.

"Spock, do you sense something different about the ship? The people, I mean. They're . . . quieter. More polite in a . . . in an abstract way, almost. I asked McCoy and he said he hadn't noticed anything. But he, too, seemed . . . well . . . distant—as if he were thinking of something else." He cocked an eyebrow at the Vulcan. "You observe everything, Spock."

"As an outsider, you mean?"

"Your . . . Vulcan heritage does give you a certain perspective. There's nothing I can put my finger on, but . . ." He shrugged again. "There's *something*. It's something I'm missing." He pointed a finger at Spock. "I recognize *part* of it. That feeling you get just before you go into combat. But there's nothing at Omicron Theta. I know just a scout ship has visited there, but the natives are at about European medieval social and technological level, six or eight points on the human scale. Nothing extraordinary."

"But?"

"But what? But I don't know. There's *something* going on, I feel it. The crew . . . they're distant." He frowned at Spock. "Did I do something—or *not* do something—that is irritating them?"

"Not that I'm aware of, Admiral."

"There's *something* going on, Mister Spock. Think about it. Find out for me."

"Yes, Admiral."

"Admiral Kirk, please report to the shuttlecraft airlock area."

Kirk broke his stride along a corridor and banged on the wall intercom. "This is Kirk. Who wants me?"

"Commander Spock, sir."

"Very well. Kirk out." He banged the stud again and turned toward the nearest turbolift, frowning.

"All right, Spock, what is it? Have you—"

The Vulcan held up his hand in a warning signal and Kirk choked off his question. "Admiral, there seems to be a confusion about the safety procedure in this airlock. Would you inspect it, sir?"

"Spock, that's the duty of the chief engineer."

"He's busy, sir, and it would only take a moment."

Kirk looked at his first officer, and seeing something in his manner, he entered the lock and the thick door cycled close behind him. He saw that the lock intercom had been sabotaged and was useless. He turned to the Vulcan, raising his eyebrows.

"We cannot be overheard here," Spock said. "Admiral, you were right, there is something going on. Mutiny."

"Mutiny!" Kirk was shocked. "These are Starfleet people, these are people I've—"

Spock again held up a warning hand. "Nevertheless, it is my belief something sinister is happening here. For one thing we are not going to Omicron Theta." Kirk blinked in surprise. "We are due to arrive at Psi Nu Alpha within six hours."

Kirk searched his memory. "Isn't that where the Sisters of the Sacred Heart have a monastery?"

"Yes, there's a small Terran colony there as well. It is well out of the normal trade routes. In fact, it has only one interesting aspect: it is the closest planet with an intelligent population to Marris V."

Kirk stared at the wall a moment. "But why would anyone here want to go there? It's a rather bleak place, isn't it?"

"Yes, by Terran terms. It's called St. Sebastian by the colonists and, indeed, it is desolate, about on the level of Earth during the Posthomic period of the Cenozoic, when mammals were just beginning to proliferate. Really quite primitive."

Kirk chewed at his lip. "Why there?"

"I do not know, Admiral. Would you like me to speculate?"

"Please, Spock."

"The only factor which seems to me important is that of distance. That is, it is simply the nearest planet with intelligent life to Marris V. And there is another factor: I believe you and I, sir, are the only ones left untouched."

"Untouched? Untouched by what?"

"I do not know, Admiral, but I suspect a virus of some particular malignancy."

Kirk said, "But . . . but everyone seems so . . ."

"So normal, Admiral? You were the one who pointed out the feeling of difference. I merely tested and extrapolated. Whatever the personnel of the *Enterprise* are, they are no longer wholly human."

"Then why am I not . . ." He fell silent and looked at Spock in shock. "But how do you *know* I am normal, or—"

"Or how do you know *I* am normal, Admiral? By logic, of course, and peripheral data. You, to my mind, are *not* different. I have tested several members of your crew; they *are* different, but in a way I cannot exactly determine. Not robotlike, not zombies, but they seem to possess a single-mindedness to the point of only minor functioning ability on the periphery of their awareness. I deliberately baited Doctor McCoy and he refused the opportunity for one of his celebrated acid statements."

"*Bones?* It's affected *McCoy?*"

"I'm afraid so, Admiral. Which brings us to . . . us. I am a Vulcan, my body chemistry is different. I am not subject to some of the hazards those of human blood face. But you are, undeniably, of human origin, yet you do not seem to be affected. Question: why?"

Kirk blinked. "I'm perfectly normal in every . . ." He stopped. "Left-handed, right-handed sugars!" Quickly, he explained to Spock what McCoy had done.

"That must explain your apparent immunity, Admiral." He paused, thinking. "Which means you have approximately twelve or thirteen hours of immunity at the outside."

"But what can we do?"

"They still obey you, do they not?"

"Yes," Kirk said, "but if I order them to do something they don't want to do . . ." His voice trailed off. "Command, Spock, is a fragile thing. Ideally, men and women follow you because they want to, that they see a sensible reason to do so. It might be a matter of life and death, that they feel their best chance is with you. Or that you represent something they believe in enough to risk and perhaps even give their lives for. You may represent an ideal, a philosophical or social belief."

"Less ideally, you are power. If they don't follow you, something dire will happen. But if the crew is affected in some way, they must have a different set of priorities."

"Admiral, what are the first conditions of any infection?"

"To identify, then isolate. Then, of course, to cure."

"We have identified only in that we know something has affected the entire crew—except you and myself. We must isolate the infection then. We cannot get within transporter or shuttlecraft range of St. Sebastian."

Kirk looked at him with growing horror. "It would spread, whatever it is." He shook his head angrily.

"If you carry that to the ultimate conclusion it means we destroy the *Enterprise*, and as soon as possible."

"That is a possibility, Admiral."

"A final one, Spock. Surely things are not that bad? Perhaps an infection has spread. Maybe it has only made the sick ones distant, uh, self-involved . . ."

"Then why the secret diversion to St. Sebastian, sir?"

"Uh . . . I have no answer for that. It's hardly a liberty port. We are out here at the edge of unexplored territory. After Omicron Theta it's all uncharted."

"Exactly, Admiral. That way is unknown, but back toward the Federation centers there are people. Lots of people. Many races, billions of individuals."

Kirk's face grew hard. "Something on Marris V got aboard. But there's never been anything intelligent reported on that marsh planet."

"It does not have to be intelligent, sir, to spread. All virus diseases simply *feed*. They multiply as long as there is a supply of hosts."

"And the crew knew there was a human colony on this St. Sebastian. That means whatever this is, it can read minds."

"Perhaps it becomes symbiotic with the host. If it took over a Terran cow, for example, it would only be able to tap the rather bucolic memories of the cow. If it overpowers a human it has those memories available. And all aboard know of the library computer and how to contact it and extract non-classified information. And there are some aboard who know how to get at classified information as well."

"McCoy . . . Scott . . . Uhura . . . Sulu . . . Chekov . . . you, me . . . Leslie, to some extent." Kirk looked stricken. "They know everything. The self-destruct mechanism, the Ultra Purple codes, the security devices, the defense screens . . ."

"Knowing and using are two different matters, Admiral. My estimation is that whatever controls the crew is on a simple mission of survival. Perhaps it evolved on Marris—or came there from somewhere else—and used the life forms there as hosts. But now it has more mobile hosts, and it will seek to spread."

"Plague!"

"In a sense. There would be no loss of life—just control. As long as the virus, or bacteria, or whatever it is, was allowed to spread, then things would be left to proceed as normal. But if it was thwarted . . ." Spock hesitated. "This is all speculation, Jim, but this must be a primitive mechanism. It might simply use pain to achieve its ends. If it controls the body as fully as I suspect it might, it could cause unbearable pain to the host."

Kirk was silent. "I would suspect a subwarp message to Starfleet would not be sent. If we somehow managed to trigger the self-destruct mechanism that would still not solve the problem of whatever it is which may be left on Marris V. If we do not stop the *Enterprise* before St. Sebastian, it will spread and from there to . . . to everywhere."

"That is a reasonable estimate of the situation, sir.

The only factors to add to that equation are you and me. We are still in control of ourselves."

"For another twelve hours or so, at least," Kirk said. "Even if we did do something, they could immobilize us. Even kill us, before we completed whatever it is we are going to do." He grinned suddenly at Spock. "We are, of course, going to do something, aren't we, Mister Spock?"

"A logical assumption, Admiral. If we assume that this invading virus can command the deductive powers of its host, we then must assume we are fighting our own friends at or near the peak of their reasoning abilities. Which means they must have already disabled the self-destruct mechanism. They will then attempt to isolate or immobilize us the moment they suspect we are not cooperating."

"Which is why we met in here, in an airlock."

"Exactly, Admiral. Do you have any suggestions?"

"No," he breathed. "Do you?"

"Yes. We need data. I propose we isolate one of the infected members and determine the nature of the random factor here."

"Whom do you have in mind?"

"Doctor McCoy. And here is how I propose we do it."

"Doctor McCoy, would you examine Admiral Kirk, please?"

McCoy turned from a blank screen and looked at Spock and Kirk in the doorway. Kirk looked weak and confused. "What is the matter?" he asked, getting up slowly.

"I don't know," Kirk said. "It's embarrassing, but I have these . . . these strange sensations . . ."

"Get on the diagnostic table, Admiral."

"Doctor, may I suggest privacy?" Spock said. "He is, after all, of flag rank."

"Yes, of course," McCoy said. He thumbed a switch. "This is Doctor McCoy: I wish to have my lab isolated for a short time, during an examination. Quarantine One in effect."

"Yes, sir," replied the recorded voice of the computer. The hatches slid shut and locked.

"Now, Admiral, if you'll—"

Spock used the Vulcan nerve-pinch to shock McCoy into unconsciousness. He placed him on the diagnostic table planned for Kirk, and after a few moments' study of the electronic charts, turned to Kirk. "He has two degrees of fever, his heartbeat is seven percent faster than normal. Metabolic rate up twelve point five percent, and his blood pressure is up as well. He's sick, but only slightly sick in a way."

"But what's *wrong* with him?" Kirk demanded.

Spock picked up a blood analyzer unit and pressed it into McCoy's neck. It hissed, and then he plugged the entire unit into the main unit and flicked on a screen.

The Vulcan's dark eyes narrowed. He pointed with a long bony finger at some nondescript blobs pulsing through the blood sample. "Those are not natural to human blood."

"What are they?"

Spock flicked the magnifier higher, his eyes intent on the screen. "I don't know yet, Admiral."

"Find out, Spock," Kirk said, looking at the closed hatch. Would they get suspicious? he wondered. He also looked at the camera pickups. "I have an idea," he said. He took the unconscious McCoy from the bed and sat him carefully in a chair, propping him up and leaning his head forward so that he appeared to be looking into a microscope. Then he hopped up on the diagnostic table and stretched out to wait.

"What we observed in Doctor McCoy's blood," Spock said, turning from the analyzer unit, "seem to be a rather unusual form of phytoplankton. Those are single-celled plants which form the base of the food chain. They are eaten by larger plankton, which are eaten by fish, which in turn are eaten by larger fish and so on."

"But how did they get aboard?" Kirk asked, sitting up. "We have some pretty tough decontamination methods."

"Either someone was sloppy, equipment was defective, or . . . it was deliberate," Spock outlined.

"All right," Kirk said, getting down and pacing. "First—how do we kill it? Second—how did it get aboard? If we kill the existing . . ." He turned to Spock.

"Phytoplankton, Admiral."

"How do you know there isn't more, somewhere?"

"Suggest one thing at a time. I will investigate how it got aboard first."

"What do I do?" Kirk asked.

"I would suggest you go about business as usual, captaining the ship."

Kirk cocked an eyebrow at his science officer. "You know, Spock, that makes me sound a bit like a figurehead."

"There is nothing wrong with that, Admiral. If you have properly trained personnel within a functioning structure it should be able to get along without you very well."

Kirk looked at him again. "Are you certain that is the answer I want to hear?"

Spock shrugged. "It is self-evident. If it were not so, you would be at the control center on the bridge at all times."

"All right, Spock, all right. I'll go around 'showing the flag' as they used to say . . . and make no changes which will disturb them."

"Excellent, Admiral. Now may I suggest you stay here until Doctor McCoy awakens? He might have some questions about why he was rendered unconscious by a fellow officer." Spock turned toward the computer terminal.

The screen listed the *Enterprise* personnel who had gone to the surface of Marris V: Galloway, the security chief, and three others, Friedman, Merlino, and Pearson; Admiral James T. Kirk; Lieutenant Commander Sulu in a separate transportation. Spock touched a communicator stud.

"Transporter Room. Lieutenant Commander Leslie, please."

"Leslie."

"This is Spock. When Mister Sulu came aboard, did he go through standard decon procedures?"

"Oh, yes, sir. Sulu . . . uh, Mister Sulu is very careful. He brings up a lot of samples and things for his collection, and he's very conscientious about that, very aware. Why, sir?"

"He was alone?"

"Yes, sir. We brought him up direct from some swamp."

"Thank you, Mister Leslie. Spock out."

The Vulcan's brow furrowed in thought. He ignored the awakening doctor, and removed the blood sample from the analyzer.

"It was an accident, Bones, Spock didn't mean it. He apologizes."

McCoy was rubbing his neck but he didn't seem particularly disturbed. He looked at Spock and shrugged. But his attitude did disturb Kirk, who quickly took Spock from the un-quarantined sickbay.

Walking along the curving corridor of the main section, Kirk asked an impatient question. "All right, what did you find out?"

"That Mister Sulu is the most likely candidate. Besides yourself and the security team he was the only one to go down."

Kirk stopped. "We beamed down to the manager's courtyard, which is in a sealed dome, and never left it. I only saw the swamp from a distance, through a port."

"Mister Sulu makes voluminous additions to his collection at most of the worlds we visit," Spock said. He hefted the blood sample in its tube. "I think I shall do a little experimentation."

"It's a bacteria," he told Kirk as they stood in the sealed shuttlecraft airlock. "I punched up what we had on Marris V, which is not much. A fresh-water ocean covers most of the surface, and there, perhaps, is the clue."

"Fresh water? Not salt?"

"It may not be able to survive a saline solution."

"But *blood* is salty. In fact, it's about the same level of salt as the oceans of Earth were when life crawled out of the seas."

"Perhaps that is the upper limit of tolerance. I propose we innoculate one of the victims with a saline solution. We will need to administer vitamins subcutaneously to give nutrition while the phyto-plankton is eating up everything in the blood that *isn't* salty. Then, faced with nothing *but* salty blood, it may starve to death."

Kirk looked shocked. "Spock!"

"Do you have an alternative plan, Admiral?"

Kirk took a deep breath. "Will it be safe?"

"Nothing is totally safe, Admiral. It is *reasonably* safe, yes."

Kirk nodded. "But suppose we give them the saline solution and then they become reinfected by others? It means we must isolate each one until he or she recovers."

"That means we must do it as quietly as possible until we can build a force of recovered victims."

"If the saline solution works, you mean. All right, let's do it. Two hypos, one with saline, one with vitamins."

"Mister Sulu, report to the captain's quarters," Uhura said from her station on the bridge. Sulu nodded and got up, motioning to a relief navigator to take his place.

The door hissed open and Sulu entered. "Sir?" he said, looking at Admiral Kirk. Mr. Spock was to his left. He saw Spock move and turned quickly. He saw the hypo coming at him and he struck out with the cutting edge of his hand, but Spock dodged and thrust the hypo against his chest.

There was a hissing pop and Sulu staggered back. It seemed as though his chest was on fire. His heart pumped frantically, but it only sent the saline solution through his arteries to every part of his writhing body.

Kirk stepped forward and stabbed the vitamin-loaded hypo into Sulu's arm. The young officer was yelling now, tearing at his chest. Spock leaned down and gave him the Vulcan nerve pinch. His body went limp, but here and there a muscle twitched.

They dragged him into Kirk's inner bedroom and put him on the table. Kirk thumbed the intercom. "Sickbay."

"*McCoy*," the familiar voice said.

"Bones, please come to my quarters at once."

"*Admiral, I'm very busy. Can we make it later?*"

"Doctor McCoy, that's an order. Kirk out."

Spock and Kirk looked at the bodies lying limply on the cabin floor: Sulu, McCoy, Leslie, Galloway and Glaser, who were Security officers, Yeoman Linda Chang, and Montgomery Scott.

Kirk rubbed at his shoulder. Scott had put up quite a fight, knocking the hypo from Spock's hand. None of them had regained consciousness.

"Not enough yet," Kirk said, looking at a chronometer. "And we're running out of time."

"Mister Chekov has the conn," Spock said. "If we revive Mister Sulu—"

"And if he's cured," Kirk added wryly.

"Then you and he could return to the bridge and relieve Chekov and one other." Kirk nodded and with a dubious expression helped Spock revive Hikaru Sulu.

The young man awoke and his slack features winced in pain. "Ow! I'm on fire!" Then he looked around at the reclining figures and got a puzzled expression. "Admiral, what's going on?"

"You've been ill. Now I want you to help us."

The turbolift hatch opened and Kirk and Sulu

strode onto the bridge. "I have the conn, Mister Chekov," Kirk said.

"It's all right, Keptin, I can handle it. We're almost at our destination."

"Mister Chekov, I am relieving you. Report to Doctor McCoy for your physical."

"Physical, sir? Keptin, I just—"

"Do as you are ordered, Mister Chekov. At once!" He turned toward the beautiful black woman at the communications station. "Lieutenant Commander Uhura, report to Mister Spock for special duty."

"Sir, I—"

"What has happened to discipline?" Kirk roared. "I have given you an order!"

Uhura blinked and rose, motioning over a screen monitor midshipman to take her place.

But instead of exiting through the turbolift she got behind Kirk and attacked him. With a wild, wordless scream she jumped on him and put both hands across his face. Kirk felt a tingling heat and fought back, digging an elbow into Uhura's stomach. But the maddened woman seemed possessed of super-human strength and she and Kirk fell to the floor in a tangle.

Sulu karate-chopped Chekov as the assistant navigator got up, then delivered him a kick, knocking him back. The Russian fell over the kicking legs of the two on the floor, struck his head, and went limp.

Three of the crew at stations charged Sulu. He was sent stumbling back by the weight of the bodies, but recovered and punched one of the weapons control people in the stomach, doubling her over.

Kirk fought free of Uhura's scratching hands and reluctantly put a hard fist to her jaw. She arched up and then collapsed. Kirk scrambled to his feet to use the momentum of the midshipman who came at him from Uhura's station to send him crashing into the opposite railing. The young man recovered and came back, but Kirk flipped him and knocked him unconscious. He whirled to help Sulu, but saw the young officer dispatch the last of the attackers.

They paused for a moment, surveying the carnage, and Kirk took out the saline solution hypo and Sulu brought out the more compact vitamin-loaded hypo. They methodically went from crewman to crewman, putting the hypos into their flesh.

Then Kirk said, "Computer. This is Order 101-Alpha-Omega. Seal the turbolifts to the bridge. Deactivate the auxiliary controls and prepare to execute Order 101-Beta-Omega."

"Completed. Ready to execute Order 101-Beta-Omega."

"Exception to Order 101-Beta-Omega: sickbay and the quarters of Commander Spock." The bridge was automatically exempt.

"Understand."

"Execute Order 101-Beta-Omega."

Throughout the ship hatches slammed shut and sealed. The airlocks to the exterior of the ship locked. Turbolifts stopped. And Morpheus-Nine was piped into the ventilation system. Crewmen caught at their throats, gagged, and fell over, unconscious.

Kirk looked at his chronometer. The minutes

seemed like hours, a cliché whose truth was all too painful for Admiral James T. Kirk.

"Computer—void order 101-Beta-Omega and Order 101-Alpha-Omega."

"Order completed."

"Mister Sulu, will you see to the crew with the others?"

"Aye, sir." The young officer paused. "Sir, I . . . I did follow procedures."

"I know, Mister Sulu." He turned in his chair and looked at the guilt-ridden officer. "There's always a wild card, Mr. Sulu. Sometimes more than one." He waved him on. "Go. Then come back here and set the course right."

"Aye, sir!" Sulu left and Kirk turned toward the main screen.

Stars. The stars were not endless, but for all practical purposes they might as well have been. Millions of them in any quadrant of the sky . . . and some of those points of light were *other* galaxies, with their billions of stars. And each with its secrets. Nature had created limitless variety, and all sought survival and perpetuity, as was their right.

Kirk thought: But why do they all jump on us?

Then he smiled, for he'd have it no other way.

The Secret Empire

THE star system of Omicron Theta was a wreck. Five planets orbited the Class M sun. Two were distant gas giants, one a near-molten ball close to the star, and two were seared, lifeless worlds. Three long, thin belts of shattered rock circled the sun where planets had once turned.

"Natural disaster or . . . war?" Kirk asked.

"My readings indicate an atomic war of immense magnitude, Admiral—enough to tear planets apart."

"Radiation?"

"Minimal. The wars were well over a thousand years ago."

Kirk sighed. "Well, I suppose we should give them

a quick survey, as long as we are here, then move on. Mr. Spock, would you like to head the party? Either one of those ruined worlds would be enough, I think. We'll leave the rest for the scout ships."

"Yes, Admiral, I'd be most interested. The outermost of the two ruined planets would be the more appropriate."

"Mr. Chekov, put us in orbit." He thumbed a stud. "Transporter Room, prepare to beam down a party." He grinned at the Vulcan. "Good luck, Mr. Spock."

The Vulcan raised his eyebrow. "Luck, Admiral, is no substitute for preparedness."

The surface of Omicron Theta V was a bleak, nearly airless land where only tortured scrubs of grayish bushes grew. There were lakes of molten glass as large as American states, and vast deserts of seared soil and shattered mountains. There was no life, and only a weak, fitful wind stirred the sands.

Five shafts of light were the first new thing which had appeared on the surface of the cratered planet in over a thousand years. The light sparkled and took shape and five stood on the smooth surface, bulky in their spacesuits.

"Mr. Sulu, collect what biological specimens you can," Spock said over his suit radio. "Sergeant Galloway, establish a lookout post. That hummock should do. Midshipman Chang, document the tricorder readings."

"And me?" Lieutenant Commander Uhura asked.

"Basic observation, Commander. See what you can see. We meet here in one hour."

"Aye, sir," they all said and separated to explore.

Forty minutes later Uhura looked at her wrist chronometer and estimated how long it would take to return. She had been wandering through the crevices and folds of the melted landscape, finding little. Here and there was some unmarked feature of the old landscape, sheltered by a cliff or outcropping, but it told her little.

She turned to go back and took another slippery gulley, which promised to come approximately back toward the prominence where they had beamed down. The walking was difficult in the suit, as she could not see her feet all that clearly, and the ground was glassy with flamed soil.

Uhura rounded a corner and gasped as she saw a hunch-backed shadow, then gave a great sigh of relief as she realized it was Spock in his cumbersome space suit. "You frightened me," she admitted.

Spock did not answer, and she looked at what he was looking at. A little way off, sheltered in a fold of rock, was an artificial structure, a masonry block, with a low, square doorway. On top of the block was a pair of feet, carved in stone, and sheared off just above the huge ankles.

"What is it?" she asked, excited and expectant.

"A monument from whatever ancient race once lived here," Spock said. "Notice the doorway. There's a bit of sand against it, but I think we can remove that with our phasers."

Without waiting for comment Spock moved forward, adjusting his phaser to distintegrate, but with a limited range. His weapon sent out a fiery ray which sparked over the sand, dissolving it away in layers until the door was relatively free of the impeding sand.

Spock pressed against the door in the stone opening, but could not budge it. Uhura helped, but neither could move the metal door, which was corroded and warped. Spock looked at his watch, then lifted his phaser.

The door vibrated into nothingness and dust swirled out. Spock turned on his helmet light and looked in, stepping through a moment later. Uhura looked nervously around. "Mr. Spock?" she said. "What do you see?"

"An interesting passage, slanting sharply down," he replied. "Inform the ship I shall investigate for ten minutes, then return."

"Uh, Mr. Spock, may I come with you?"

"If you wish."

Uhura reported to the *Enterprise*, and Captain Kirk replied, "Don't stay too long and don't go too deep."

"Aye, sir," she said and went into the base of the huge ruined statue.

The walls were of large blocks of native stone, ruptured here and there, as if by an earthquake. A few feet inside, the floor slanted sharply down and a few feet beyond that one wall and part of the ceiling had totally collapsed, spreading stone, rough rocks, and dirt over the narrow floor. Uhura hurried on and soon caught up with Spock.

"What is this place?"

"Unknown," he replied. "Perhaps some kind of secret or seldom-used passage to the surface from some ancient underground structure."

"It's spooky," she said.

"Hardly a scientific description," Spock said dryly.

The passage turned and there were steps down, then more turnings and more steps. Here and there the smooth stones were absent and the roughly hewn walls of natural rock were seen. The steps and turnings seemed endless, and Uhura was already thinking of the long climb back.

"Mr. Spock, it's about time we went back," she radioed.

"Um. Look, a room of some sort."

The steps led into a small, stone-walled room with thick dust on the floor and a rusted piece of metal leaning against the wall. "That looks like a . . . a spear," Uhura said.

"Interesting, but we have run out of time," Spock said. He looked into one of the two passages leading from the room, flashing his helmet light downward. He had turned toward the other passage when out of the dark passage charged a half-dozen shrilly chittering creatures like monstrously large insects, spears flashing in the helmet light.

Uhura screamed and reached for her phaser. It was set on stun and she downed one of the creatures before she was knocked over. Her head hit the back of her helmet and she was knocked unconscious.

Spock had his phaser on Kill but he did not use it. He struck out at one of the attackers with a gloved fist, sending it crashing against the wall, where it toppled forward limply. But the others smashed into Spock, bearing him down.

Uhura awoke and immediately her senses were assaulted. *Smells:* something like onion, sweet, oil, a touch of some spice, and a rather sickening perfume. *Noises:* Clucks, hums, a low throbbing, an echoing cry, a voice saying something she didn't understand.

She opened her eyes. She lay on a rather dirty floor of some cold concretelike material. Her protective spacesuit was gone, as was her outer uniform. Her phaser, communicator, and other gear were also missing.

Two creatures like giant erect cockroaches stood looking at her with eyes on stalks. They were the size of a small human and had slim metal spears. A narrow metal collar circled each thorax but they were otherwise without clothing.

Carefully Uhura sat up, her eyes on the cockroach-like creatures, her stomach churning in disgust. *Careful*, she thought. They are intelligent—the spears show a use of tools.

She put her back against the concrete wall and got very slowly to her feet. It was cool in the corridor, but not cold. A cockroach came out of a nearby passageway and walked by with a kind of hopping motion, one eye stalk swiveling to look at Uhura.

Don't think of them as cockroaches, Uhura thought. That might trap you into a line of thinking that could be fatal. She looked around. "Mr. Spock?" she said softly. The tendrils atop the "cockroaches" twitched, but they didn't move. "Mr. Spock!" she said louder. One of the cockroaches shifted position, but neither of them said or did anything.

Uhura started edging along the wall toward the passageway to her left. The cockroach guards calmly moved along with her, keeping her within striking distance of their spears. Uhura looked around the corner and saw Commander Spock standing tall amid a dozen or so of the cockroaches. He seemed to be working on something.

"Mis . . . Mister Spock?"

The Vulcan looked at her. A dozen pairs of stalked eyes also turned to look, and Uhura gulped. "Ah, Ms. Uhura, you are well? I gave you a brief examination earlier and you seemed basically unharmed."

"I . . . I have a headache, but . . ." She waved at the cockroaches. "What . . . what are these?"

"As yet undetermined," Spock said. The cockroaches moved, and Uhura saw that Spock was wearing only his Vulcan inner heating garment. To the Vulcan, raised on that planet's 140-degree mean temperature, these cool underground passages must be icy. Spock pointed. "Your clothes are there. We were searched for weapons."

Uhura shivered, thinking of the thin, delicate mandibles of the cockroaches touching her. She saw her uniform and went slowly to it and dressed quickly. "What are you working on?" Again, the stalked eyeballs turned in her direction.

"A universal-translator. Although this hand-carried unit has a link to the ship's computer, it's quite limited. But I'm trying to adapt it."

"They . . . they talk?" Uhura realized she had not heard them say anything.

"Naturally."

"How do they know that is what you're doing?" she asked, doing up the last fastening in her sleekly tailored uniform and feeling much better for it.

"They don't, but I have proceeded openly and cautiously." He clicked something in place and spoke into the device. "Greetings, we come in peace."

At the same time, with only a momentary lag, the translator's speaker let out a chittering which caused the dozen or so cockroachelike creatures to step back in alarm. "Do not fear," Spock said slowly and distinctly. "We mean you no harm."

There was a sudden burst of chittering from almost all of the cockroaches, and the translator blinked red. Spock held up his hand and stood motionless until they all stopped. Then he held the machine toward the nearest of the creatures, saying, "You speak."

A shrill chittering was quickly translated into a rather harsh, garbled, accented voice, saying, "Who are you, tallones? How can you be skinned and live?"

For the first time Uhura felt like laughing, but she stifled the impulse. Solemnly, Spock said, "Those were protective garments. We are from the United Federation of Planets. Our starship, the U.S.S. *Enterprise,* is in orbit above this world."

The cockroaches stirred angrily and there was a wild swaying of long antennae and a tense gripping of thin spears. Uhura backed up, looking around for her phaser and communicator.

The translator blinked red again as the cockroaches all chittered at once, then finally one of them seemed to shout down the others. "—to the masters! We take them for justice to the masters!"

There was much milling around, but the swaying eyestalks were very curious as Spock calmly donned his uniform, ignoring the stabbing motions of the spears. He looked at Uhura and motioned with a tilt of his head.

They went out into the passage, surrounded by the chest-high mob of brown creatures. Uhura could examine them more closely as they walked briskly along, but didn't really want to. Outside of admiring a dark-brown chitinous carapace and very strong but thin legs and "arms" she had no taste for the creatures. *Why do they have to look like cockroaches, of all things?"* she thought.

They went down stairs and ramps and long slanting corridors. The walls were sometimes roughly hewn blocks of stone, sometimes rather crudely poured concrete, and sometimes the natural rock of caverns and caves. They passed many branching corridors, past rooms and caverns filled with an odd variety of things.

One great cavern was a kind of farm, with purple-gray plants growing under amber lights and producing great yellowing melonlike fruit. Another room was filled with whitish cubes of some kind of compressed vegetable material. A long passage contained many small rooms, stacked with dull red cylinders of a claylike substance, yellow strips rolls in big loops, or bales of purple-gray leaves.

They saw an underground lake or pool of a dark green liquid, and a cavern where a hundred cockroaches attended to a "field" of bright green plants with tiny red berries, brightly lit by a bank of yellow lights.

Then the corridor walls seemed smoother, cleaner, and more regular. The cockroaches they met were without spears, but seemed to have more authority. There was almost a fight between the spear-carrying roaches and a band of new ones, wearing a knotted red string around their carapaces. At last they were allowed to proceed, but with only five of the spear-carriers going with them.

They came to a guarded door and were allowed through, and Uhura's eyes opened in surprise. It was warmer here, with high arched corridors and spacious rooms with furniture. A wall screen in one room was displaying a complex geometric pattern of moving color. Cockroaches passed by with metal bowls of yellow puffballs or small dark berries.

But it was the inhabitants which surprised both Spock and Uhura. Uhura, at least, had been expecting more of the cockroaches, but instead she saw several totally new creatures: small humanoids with burnished dark skin, high foreheads, and thick ponytails of black hair. They were obviously mammals and wore colorful clothing in many hues.

The first one who saw them exclaimed something in a high, piping yell, and the translator said: "Gods of Malphor! Giants!"

Several of them gathered and crowded close, touching both Spock and Uhura, chattering, their eyes bright with excitement. The translator, overloaded with too many words, just blinked red again.

"Mr. Spock . . ."

"You are an officer in Starfleet, Lieutenant Commander Uhura, and you are expected to act like one."

"Fine," she said, "but how are you supposed to act?"

"Dignified," he replied. Uhura gave him a hard look. Easy for you, she thought. You're always dignified.

Their little band grew at every intersection, with more of the well-formed but diminutive humanoids joining them. The chatter was shrill and incomprehensible. Then they came to the big metal doors where, for the first time, there were humanoid guards.

They conversed for a few moments with the cockroaches, and then the doors were opened. "An airlock," Uhura said, looking around her. The first door closed behind them. The guards eyed them with a mixture of hatred, curiosity, fear, and what Uhura could only interpret as a kind of attraction.

The inner airlock opened and they were in a much more richly decorated section. The ceilings were higher and the walls made of a beautifully patterned stone. Tapestries hung from the walls and Uhura saw Spock studying them as they passed. The imagery was not very realistic by Terran standards, more given to symbols and colors than actual figures, though there were some.

"Fascinating," Spock said to her. "I think this indicates a long rivalry between the inhabitants of this planet and another race. They spread out to other planets and there were wars over the disputed worlds . . . culminating in the destruction of several."

"Who won?"

Spock shrugged. "Who wins any war fought with atomic weapons? There were no winners and the remnants live here, in what was once a fort, or perhaps a royal bomb shelter."

"And these . . creatures?" she said, indicating the cockroachlike guards.

"Look at that tapestry." A single humanoid figure stood atop a pile of what appeared to be dead or submissive cockroaches. "A slave race, perhaps bred from prisoners of war."

Uhura shivered and then they were at a tall, curtained entrance. Humanoid guards opened the curtains and they were ushered through.

It was a large room, with a strange floor that was

not flat but instead rose and fell gently, smoothly, to pinnacles and hollows. Atop one of the pinnacles was a cluster of thrones, with built-in tables piled with what Uhura assumed were fruit. Statuary was tightly pressed into the cluster, as was a stone pot with a small, brightly colored bush growing in it. In each throne was a humanoid figure, a miniature human dressed in silks and jewels, with many rings, bracelets, necklaces, and earrings, which were worn by both sexes.

At the top was a rather fat individual, with a young and pretty female on either side. Just below him sat a resplendent female with a muscular young male on either side.

"Barik, what have you found?"

"Lord of the Cavern, Most Gracious King of the Inner Chamber, Victorious Monarch of the Eight Worlds, Destroyer of the Slow-witted Insects, Pre-determined Leader of—"

"Barik, never mind that! Who are these giants?"

"Invaders, Most Majestic of all the Great Kings. The outer guards captured them, O Singer of the Great Victory Songs, the—"

"Be silent, Barik. Giants, come closer!" Spock and Uhura moved carefully through the surrounding mob of cockroaches and nobles. "Ah . . ." the king said. "Striking. Outrageously large, but—"

The queen, or who Uhura assumed was a queen-like person, spoke up. "The male has pointed ears! The giant has pointed ears." For some reason that seemed to cause a wave of tittering laughter. Spock merely looked at them with a raised eyebrow.

"Quiet!" the king ordered. "Who are you, invaders? Why have you come here?"

"Oh, Great Monarch of the Citadel of Safety," Barik said. "Bringer of Safe Walls and Water, the *chitik* say they are from a starship—"

A gasp came over all the humanoids in the throne room. From his tower of thrones, the king spoke sharply. "I asked the dark giant, Barik! You," he said, pointing a beringed finger at Spock. "Is this true?"

"Your Majesty," Spock began, giving a slight bow. "It is true. We are officers from a starship sent by a great empire to contact you. I am Ambassador Spock and this is Ambassador Uhura. We have come to rescue you."

There was a hissing of breath and the king looked angry. "Rescue us! We do not need rescue, Ambassador! We have lived here for two thousand years! We are comfortable, we command, we rule the eight planets of Tarachi!"

"Majesty, there are only five and—"

"Stop!" The king's voice thundered out. "You lie! We rule over eight worlds!"

"He, he speaks truth, Majesty," Uhura said. "Two are shattered into debris and this planet and another are lifeless and—"

"No!" the king bellowed, standing. The hands of the slave girls reached for him but he slapped them away. Outraged, he screamed in anger. "I rule! I, Bedallion the Forty-first! *I* rule the eight worlds! We won the Second Great War! We defeated the *chitik!* Look at them now—*slaves!*"

"Nevertheless," Spock said calmly, "all the planets once capable of life are destroyed or lifeless."

"No!" King Bedallion bellowed, "You lie! You *lie!*" He fell back onto his throne, to be caressed and kissed.

"Majesty, if you were to return to us a certain device," Spock said. "I could demonstrate the truth of what I say."

"What?" The Queen stood. "How can one demonstrate an untruth?"

"One cannot, Majesty," Spock said, giving her a slight bow. "But one *can* demonstrate a *truth.*"

"How?" she said haughtily. "Not even the Makers of Dreams can do that." Her eyes narrowed. "Are you a secret Maker?"

"No, Majesty, merely an ambassador from a great empire who wishes only to learn."

She seemed mollified and sat down. "We will think of this. Bedallion?"

"Uh? Yes, indeed. We must think of this. Take them away," he said. "Give them food and watch them."

"Yes, Giver of Air," Barik said. "At once, Prince of Stars, Protector of the Green, the—"

The king made a rude noise and so did the Universal-translator. They took Spock and Uhura away to a well-guarded room not far away.

There were rose-stone walls, a tapestry depicting the hand-to-hand combat between a king and a giant cockroach, a bowl of yellow fruit, and a great low bed. Uhura looked at Spock as they were alone.

"Turn it off," she said, pointing at the translator. "We can't be overheard that way."

Spock snapped the device off. "Yes?"

"You lied to them, Mr. Spock. I thought Vulcans did not lie."

"I did not lie. The first contact of any species means that those coming *are* ambassadors. And is the Federation *not* a great empire?"

"Okay, Mr. Spock—you certainly do seek to learn. But coming to rescue them—?"

"They are living in a dead-end society, one based on slave labor. No society like that has lasted. We can transport them to new worlds, giving each a new start. I used the terms I did so that they would be within the range of their understanding. If we can recover our communicators, we can do all that."

"I get the feeling they want to stay as they are," Uhura said.

"All societies resist change. I have no desire to violate the Prime Directive. We will make a case for immigration and let them decide."

"But what if—"

They were interrupted by a humanoid noble. Spock turned on the translator. He smiled oddly and gave a slight bow. "Ambassador Oohurra?"

"Uhura. Yes?"

"The Great Soverign of the Inner World has sent me to bring you to him."

Uhura looked at Spock, then said, "Why?"

The noble shrugged. "The Zamorin of the Chitik Slaves does but speak and I obey."

"Shall I?" Uhura asked Spock. He nodded absently, which made the young officer a bit angry. "Very well. Lead on, McDuff."

"My name is Count Aalvik, Ambassador," the small humanoid said, puzzled.

"You'll need this," Spock said, handing her the translator.

She took it and followed the count. They went passed the throne room, down some wide, curving steps, and to the ornate doors of private quarters. Uhura was beginning to get nervous.

King Bedallion was waiting for her alone. He dismissed Count Aalvik at once. "How is it you understand us and we you?" he asked, and she showed him the translator. "Excellent! Yours must be a great empire! Come, sit here beside me."

He was sitting on a wide couch covered in multicolored fur. He poured her a crystal glass of some yellow liquid, but she refused. "Please, Your Majesty, I am not being rude, but it would be dangerous for me to consume untested food or drink. It might even be dangerous for me to breath this air . . . or for you to breathe the same air as I do. There are diseases we—"

The king waved all that aside as nonsense, but he put down the glass. He looked her over critically. "I have never seen one like you before. You are distressingly large. Grotesque even, yet . . . yet I am attracted to you."

Uhura concealed her amusement, for the king was half her size, although perfectly proportioned.

"Thank you, Your Majesty," she said, evading his hands gracefully. "But as ambassador I am forbidden to . . . to have anything to do with those I am dealing with."

King Bedallion's face fell in disappointment. "You were . . . you were such a challenge," he sighed. "Oh, it's not easy being king here. It's the same thing year after year, you know. Nothing much new happens. I must decree all the fads, you know. We'd be *really* bored if we didn't have fads."

He jumped down from the bed and strode around. "Last year it was shaven heads and Cor designs painted on. Year before, the ten-year-cycle of nudity, excepting jewelry, of course. Three years ago, the cave-bear fad. Next year . . ." He sighed again. "It's the yellow cycle. So boring, but it's traditional."

"How can it be a fad if it's traditional?" Uhura asked.

"Because we must feign surprise, or it's no fun at all. Are you absolutely certain your duties will not let you, um, cavort a little?"

"Oh, absolutely," she said solemnly. "You know, Your Majesty, if you would restore our communicators to us—those are the little metal boxes that fit in your hand—we could show you some extraordinary sights that—"

"No, no, I know ambassadors. The second King Bedallion, he let the *chitik* ambassador into the palace—oh, it was such a great palace, too, on the shores of a lake—and that ambassador *ruined* the power-thing that kept the guardians in the sky."

Abruptly, the king turned to Uhura. "You've been there yourself. What *is* sky?"

"Uh . . . it's, um, it's the atmospheric envelope that covers a planet. The gases of the atmosphere which one breathes. It's thickest at the bottom, at the surface, and gets thinner and thinner as you go up, until there are no gases and that's space."

Bedallion looked at her suspiciously. "It gets *thinner?* Magician Thrumwald says it gets *thicker* and that is what holds the planets in their places."

Uhura blinked. "Uh . . . no, I'm afraid not."

"Good, old Thrumwald is an idiot. Always telling me we are the last, that we must do something about the food synthesizers." Bedallion kicked at the bed. "Old fool. Wait until I tell him what you said."

"Um, Your Majesty, he may be right about the, uh, the other things. I imagine you are the last. Mr., uh, Ambassador Spock was right. Two of your planets are shattered. Just orbiting rock. And this planet and another are cratered incredibly. We—"

"Stop!" He turned and shouted. "Guards!"

Humanoid guards trotted in, thin spears at the ready. "Take this . . . this giant back to her room. She bores me. She tells me truth and lies all mixed up! How can I decide which is real?"

"Your Highness, I—"

But Uhura was all but carried back to the room where they had left Spock. Discouraged, she recounted what had happened.

"We must find those communicators," he said. "The king mentioned a magician? I wonder if he might not be a kind of hereditary technician. Let us go see."

Spock rose and Uhura sat up in surprise. "The guards, Mr. Spock, they—" She heard two bodies plop onto the floor with a rattle of equipment.

"Come," Spock said, looking back through the curtain.

Uhura followed him, stepping over the two unconscious guards, who reminded her of sleeping children in dress-up. They hurried along until they ran into a surprised noble. "Noble sir," Spock said, bowing. "Might you tell me where the quarters of the Magician Thrumwald might be?"

The noble looked at them suspiciously. "You don't frighten me, you great hulks."

"I assure you, sir, we have no intention of frightening you. However, we have urgent business with Magician Thrumwald."

"Well, he certainly doesn't live in the palace. Try the slave quarters. I heard once he lived somewhere in there. Why do you want to see *him*, anyway? He's just a magician."

"Urgent business," Spock said.

"Sent by the king," Uhura added.

"Oh, very well." The small humanoid turned and pointed. "Down that way. Green door on the left. Mind you, bathe when you come back."

"Most assuredly," Uhura said, setting off after the long-legged Spock. "Definitely."

The green door was unguarded on the palace side, but there were rather large cockroach-guards on the other side. They did not say or do anything as Spock and Uhura came through. "The quarters of the Magician Thrumwald," Spock demanded. They pointed with their spears, their eyestalks swaying.

After a long walk and numerous inquiries they found a bridge across a cavern and a masonry tower on the other side, a square-built structure of black stone without windows except for the highest levels.

The bridge, however, was guarded. "What is that?" Uhura gasped. Sitting in the middle of the bridge was what seemed to be a cross between the galaxy's largest caterpillar and an armored beetle.

"Metaphorically, it's a dragon," Spock said.

"And just what—metaphorically—are you going to do about it?" Uhura asked.

"Commander, the proper question is what are we going to do about it?"

"Correction noted," she said wryly. "Uh-oh, it notices us."

"That is what it is supposed to do," Spock said. He stepped out confidently onto the bridge. The great armored caterpillar rippled and lifted a third of its length into the air. It towered above them by three times their height, but Spock just kept walking confidently toward it.

"Mister Spock," Uhura wheezed. "It—"

"You there!" Spock's voice thundered, repeated in volume from the translator. The caterpillar stopped moving, except for a thicket of antennae atop its head, which kept on waving. "We wish to speak to the Magician Thrumwald!"

"Chit-chit-*click*-chot-choop-*click-click*-clonk!"
The caterpillar said, but the translator was silent. It
simply didn't have enough material upon which to
base a translation.

"Step aside!" Spock said, his voice echoing in the
cavern. Uhura saw a stirring at a curtained window
in the tower. "I must speak to the great and re-
knowned Magician Thrumwald!"

Uhura trotted from her post of concealment and
quickly spoke in a loud voice. "His fame has spread
to the great empire of the Federation, to those who
would seek his advice." She grinned up at Spock. "I
can lie better than you," she whispered.

"So it would seem, Commander Uhura," Spock
responded.

"Chit-clonk, *click-click*, ponk! Chit-chot-chit-
click, pumpf!"

"Aside!" Spock said, but the creature still loomed
over him like a shuttlecraft on end. "We bear great
news to the great Magician Thrumwald!"

"Clonk-chit-*click*-ponk-*plink*-conk-chit, *click*-
pumpf!"

The translator hummed alive and a scratchy voice
said, "No. Go. I guard. Kill. Go."

"Great guardian of the gates," Uhura said loudly.
"Only a magician as great as Thrumwald could have
such a magnificent guardian! How great must be his
powers! We must see him to praise him!"

"Don't overdo it," Spock muttered.

"Chik-*click*-ponk-chit-clak-spoop-*click-clook!*"—
"No. I must kill you now."

"Stop!" From a high window Spock and Uhura saw a hand wave. They could see a figure and heard his cry, which sounded like, "*Click*-choot-chit-pumpf-*click*-chuum!"

The great caterpillar rumbled and fumed, but edged aside enough for Spock and Uhura to get by. They went quickly across the bridge and up to the base of the isolated tower. Then, after a few moments, the wooden door creaked open and a voice said, "Come in, come in, you great hulking beasts."

As the door closed Uhura looked around to see a humanoid figure, no higher than her waist, almost an elf of a person, white-haired and dressed in black. Then the door clicked shut and the small person glared at them.

"Now what? You're those obscenely big ambassadors, aren't you? The ones that told the king all those lies? Don't deny it, I know you are. Only giants around. What do you want here? I'm ready for you, you know. I have the Spell of Invisibility ready! I'm the master of the Barbs of Annoyance! My father was the last Magician Thrumwald, you know, and he taught me everything—how to test for poisoned drink, how to create light, how to ward off strange beings by making them sneeze, how to turn *chitik* to stone, all the good stuff. Well, speak up, will you? I'm right in the middle of a test, so don't take up my time. You, you are certainly a big female, aren't you? You with this pointed-ear giant, are you? Too bad. Wouldn't mind the challenge, myself. Of course, I'm not as young as I was. Once there was a time when I, alone and armed with only a few ready-spells, could have loved my way through the Hall of the Countesses all by myself. Long time gone that. Well, come on, speak up, you—"

"We're *trying!*" Uhura snapped.

The magician looked at her in surprise. "Well, you don't have to get like that. My fourth wife, the Lady Veron of Appuldia, Mistress of the Southern Cavern, First Born Daughter of the Defender of Xannisi, she was like you. Full of surprises. Got to be a darned nuisance. No familar, comfortable routine, always a life of novelty! Too young for me, they said, and they were right, the old biddies. Now my sixth wife, the Baroness of Oental, the Queen's Mirror, she was different—as quiet as a *sulpat*, and mixed all my secret potions just right. You don't strike me as being like her, you great brown mountain of a woman. Now if you—"

"*Magician Thrumwald,*" Spock said loudly. "We are looking for our communicators. Metal boxes about this big."

"Oh, those. Dreadful, frightening things. Yes, they're here. They always bring me things they want fixed, like I'm supposed to know *everything* . . . I do, of course, but not *everything*—everything! Can't expect me to know everything about something I've never seen before. From outside, are you? Good, good. I told the king, I told his father, I told his *grandfather,* that blind old *krut,* I told them things were going to *belazz* in a basket! Closed the whole North Cavern down in Bedallian the Thirty-Eight's time, but does anyone remember? No*oooo!* They think this is the way it always was! Fools, all of them, fools. They expect me—just me, mind you, now that the ninth wife has gone—*me* to fix the power-thing. But they're afraid of me, too, the bone-heads! Won't tell me what's wrong, but I'm supposed to fix it anyway. Wasn't this way in *my* great-grandfather's time, I tell you. The kings *then* listened! That was in the days when the quakes were still bringing down the roofs and the *kruts* were roaming the caverns, looking for food. No, *then* the kings listened, but do they listen these days? No, no, they are omnipotent these kings today, great and noble in their ignorance and—"

"Magician, please!" Uhura said. "The communicators?"

"In there, in there," he said impatiently. "Go on, right through there. Up those steps, go on, go on. Watch your heads, you great mountains of meat! Go on, go on. In there, to the right. Why did you giants have to come *now?* Disrupt a person's life. Make me yell at the last *krut* that exists. It's hard to train a *krut,* you know. Very hard. My grandfather started training that one when it was still in the egg. Played him music from Skrukin's pieces, the *Triumphal March of the Rightful King* and the *Cavern Echoes* and *Memory of Surface. Kruts* love music, if you get 'em young enough. You ever train a *krut?*" he demanded of Uhura.

"What? Uh, no."

The little person looked happy. "Good. You

passed the first test. These boneheads are always bragging how they trained a wild *krut*, the fools. Liars! *That's* the only trained *krut* in the universe!"

"Our communicators?" Uhura said, grateful for a slight break. "Where are they?"

"Why? What are you going to do with them? You set up a rival magician-fief and I'll bring down the Sores of Bakar on you! I'll cause your bones to bend, I'll electrify your hair, I'll—"

"No, please, just tell us where they are," she said.

"What do I care? I'm old. There're no children to carry on. I'd like to go out in a great explosion of magic. Summon all the powers together at once, set them against each other and go out in a great flash!" He fell silent, smiling.

"The communicators?" Spock asked.

"Oh, they're over there somewhere, behind that pickled *krut* egg . . . no, no . . . to the left . . . there, that's them, right? Couldn't make head nor tail of them. My father was good with powered things. Not me. Don't have the touch. Now, purply-plants and I, ah, now that's different. If you—"

He stopped as Spock flicked open a communicator and the bleep of the sound came to him. He looked startled and grasped at a rod of twisted colored glass. "Don't come near me, you meaty hunks of alien stuff! I can defend myself! This will turn even you into jelly! Watch it now, you—!"

"Enterprise, this is Commander Spock."

"*Spock!*" It was the voice of Captain Kirk.

"*Are you in trouble, laddie?*" Commander Scott asked. "*We can beam you up in an instant!*"

"*Are you all right?*" Kirk demanded. "*Where's Uhura?*"

"We're fine, Admiral. Commander Uhura is here with me." Quickly Spock outlined the situation.

"*I think the Prime Directive gives us enough leeway to offer them the option of going or staying,*" Kirk said. "*But I don't like the slave race situation.*"

"Who is he talking to?" the magician asked in an awed voice.

"Our captain," Uhura said, pointing up. "He's out there."

"There's nothing out there," the magician snapped. "Proven fact."

"There's a starship out there," Uhura smiled. "And another home if you want."

"Why should I leave here?" he growled. "Not that I don't have my troubles. Do you know what it costs to feed a krut these days? And powdered erak horn, can you guess what they are asking? Recycled copper wire? Flum? A good grade of baarlik? No, people never think of that! They see the glamorous life, the king's court, the balls and parties, the apprentice magicians all adoring with their sweet eyes, no, that's all people see!"

"Please," Uhura said, putting a finger to her lips as she watched Spock talk to Kirk. But the magician was not to be silenced.

"And you two great buffoons come in. Do they just

run you through and that's that? No, they expect me
to take care of things. Drain your mind and turn you
to stone, that's what Belar wanted. Turn to stone?
And me without a gram of *derisk* in the whole tower.
Count Fremla, he wanted to torture you, whatever
your name is."

"Uhura."

"Yes, he was all for that . . . if I immobilized you.
Oh, yes, he loves torturing, the *cru*. And the queen,
oh, dear me, what she wanted me to do with your
pointed-eared friend, well! *Gigantus Robotus*, that's
what she wanted. The wanton! Her mother was the
same, her grandmother and *her* mother! All the
same, the whole Fernalis line, all the same. Not one
of them could splice a copper line of *frela* an *omikir*
to save their minds, but all they do is say, 'Do this for
us, Thrumwald,' and 'Do that for us, Thrumwald,
that's a dear.' It'll be a great day when the *chitik* eats
them all. Then I can devote myself to—*eeek!*"

Four columns of shimmering light appeared in the
magician's room, and he cowered back against the
wall, holding out a shaking hand, pointing his colored glass rod.

"Don't!" Uhura said, shoving at his arm. A searing
flame melted rock from the roof and it dripped out in
splatters as a security team materialized. "Sergeant
Galloway!" Uhura said. "Help me with him!"

Galloway wrested away the glass rod and started
to break it, but Spock snapped out an order to stop.
"There's too much energy in that to release at once,
Sergeant!"

"Yes, sir," Galloway said, putting the rod carefully down on a bench. He flipped open his communicator. "Second team—hop it!"

Thrumwald stared in horrified fascination as teams of armed men materialized out of the air, dressed in red uniforms. They moved downstairs and established a perimeter around the black tower. Then Admiral James T. Kirk appeared, with Dr. McCoy and young Lex Nakashima.

"Sulu has the conn," Kirk said, "Scott is ready to back us up as needed."

"That will not be necessary, Admiral," Spock said. "This show of force is mainly psychological."

Kirk looked up at the still-glowing stone ceiling, carved from great interlocked basalt blocks. But he didn't say anything, except, "Proceed Mr. Spock, this is your show."

When the security men left the black tower they were confronted by the *krut*, looming up over them, its many legs kicking and its attennae quivering. Phasers poured power into the great undulating bulk but it took a long time for the peculiar nervous system to receive a knock-out jolt. The *krut* finally subsided and rolled up in a ball and went to sleep.

Galloway wiped the perspiration from his forehead and spoke to Spock. "Any more surprises like that one, sir?"

"Surprises, yes, Sergeant; like that, no, I don't think so."

"Why do I have to go?" muttered the Magician

Thrumwald. "They see me with you and they'll think I betrayed them. Better tie my hands and put one of those odd weapons of yours to my head. After all, I have to live here after you people are gone. You have no right to compromise me like this. Insensitive monsters! All you giants are alike—unfeeling brutes, that's what you are!"

"Sergeant, after you have tied the magician's hands, gag him as well," Spock said.

"Yessir," Galloway said, grinning. "Friedman . . ."

"Oh, very well," the magician said. "But you'll be sorry. All the kingdom comes to me, sooner or later, for my advice. Why should you be different? All I want is—"

"Sergeant, the gag."

The magician shut up and Galloway didn't gag him, winking at the impassive Spock.

They crossed the bridge, edging along past the knocked-out *krut*, and entered the palace. Consternation reigned as the small creatures ran in every direction, squealing. The *chitik* hopped and trotted away before the onslaught of the giants. Here and there one tried to take a stand and was stunned by phasers and laid out in a side passage. Within minutes Spock, Uhura, and the magician, followed by an observant Admiral Kirk and a fussy Dr. McCoy, entered the throne room.

The pyramid of thrones and lesser thrones was empty, except for the top two. King Bedallion and his queen sat with stiff dignity on their thrones, unattended by any nobles or slaves. The queen managed to look frightened, excited, and angry all at the same time. Bedallion switched from shock to anger to curiosity to outraged dignity in no particular order. "Stop where you are," he shouted, his voice cracking. "You great lumbering louts are liable to break my floors!"

"Majesty," Spock said, stepping forward. "We offer transportation to a new land, a place under the stars and a new sun."

Bedallion looked surprised, then woefully shocked. "No, never! Ugh! Horrible idea! A sun, shining right down on us? No roof, no ceiling, nothing over our heads to protect us? We'd float up and out into . . . into whatever is out there!"

"I assure Your Majesty that there are many suitable, uninhabited planets. Your system here is breaking down. You do not have the ability to repair them. Your—"

"*Stop!* I will hear no more of this! We have lived here in harmony for over three hundred generations! There is no other life for us! We have everything here!"

"You have slaves," Uhura said with some heat.

"Slaves? Of course, we have slaves, you silly giant! How else does one live? How can you be a master race without a slave race?"

"Exactly," muttered Uhura.

"We would offer the *chitik* an equal opportunity, of course," Spock said. "A planet of their own, where they could develop as naturally as possible."

Bedallion looked shocked and the queen eeked.

"Do I understand you, point-eared giant, to mean that you would steal our slaves from us? But they are ours! See the metal collars they all wear? A most satisfactory pacification device." He held up his hand. "See this? All we of noble rank wear this. A touch . . ." The *Enterprise* landing party heard threshing and thin, reedy screams from the side rooms. "And all within ten *sartums* feel real pain."

"Stop!" Uhura yelled. The king looked at her from his lofty perch, raising his delicate eyebrows.

"It's the only way, you huge thing. It is an ancient maxim of our people—'Masters command as best they can and slaves obey as they must.' Surely you see the sense in that?"

"We are prepared to offer the *chitik* the choice," Spock said, impassively.

"Choice?" the queen squealed. "*Choice*? For *slaves*?"

"They are intelligent beings, Majesty," Spock said. "The Federation will insist that—"

"Curse your Federation!" the king shouted, standing. "Curse you blundering giants! You cannot deal with giants except by force! Force is the only thing you great brutes understand!" The king seized a medallion which hung from his neck, along with others, and thumbed three of the jewels.

The pyramid of thrones seemed to fall apart as the backs of a lower ring of thrones flopped inward and curious crystalline snouts protruded. Spock fired at once, disintegrating one of them, and the suddenness of it surprised everyone. The crystals glowed and each of the humans was bathed in an aura of intense pain. Their skin seemed to be on fire, their teeth hurt, their heads all ached, their muscles were knotted. Uhura screamed and fell to her knees. The security men threshed about. Galloway, Friedman, and Lieutenant Nakashima all fired right at the pulsating crystal snouts. The pyramid of thrones was lost in a cloud of steam, flashes, and exploding stone.

"Cease fire!" Kirk yelled as Spock ran straight at the pyramid. Only he and those near him had escaped the deadly ray because of his destruction of the crystal weapon. Spock bounded up the pyramid, using the thrones as steps.

King Bedallion was in shock, staring around him at the ancient center of power in ruins. Spock ripped the medallion from him and stood over him. "We will offer each of your subjects . . . and the *chitik* as well . . . an option, Your Majesty."

Bedallion stared at him, unable to speak for a long moment. "You . . . you ruined my throne. You ruined my throne."

"Everyone aboard, Mister Spock?" Admiral Kirk said from the command chair.

"Yes, Admiral. More than three-quarters of the humanoid race voted on the first ballot to move and, of course, all of the *chitik*."

"After a few lessons in what democracy means," Uhura said with a smile. "It was not an easy concept for a race bred to centuries of slavery to understand."

"Every individual seeks personal freedom," Kirk said, "once they understand it is possible. And the rest of them, Spock?"

"Once they saw most were going, they changed their vote."

"Would you believe it, sir," Uhura said. "Bedallion is acting as though it was all his idea, that he's the Savior of the People. He's announced plans to run as president, once they become established on Ayin Aleph III."

"And the *chitik*?" Kirk asked.

"They have a hive mind," Spock said. "I've selected Lam Qaf Kha II in the Alif Sector, Admiral, if you approve."

"That's a good distance from Ayin?"

"Nine light years, sir."

"Good, Spock. And the talkative Magician Thrumwald?"

"*He's* the one who brought the giant saviors into the caverns," Uhura said. "He's the one who is leading the people to the new world. . . . he says."

Kirk sighed. "Mr. Sulu, set course for Ayin Aleph III."

"Aye, sir."

"And Mister Spock . . ."

"Yes, Admiral?"

"Do you know the words of a sage of the twentieth

century? 'Democracy guarantees elections, but elections do not necessarily guarantee great leaders. The idea of choice is democracy at its best; the choice itself may be the worst.' "

"Prudent words, Admiral, but these two races must make their own way. Just as yours and mine did."

"True, Mister Spock, true. Mister Sulu, Warp One."

Intelligence Test

Pavel Chekov checked the charge in his phaser for the sixth time, causing the head of the security detail to repress a smile for the fifth time. You'd think he hadn't transported down to an unknown planet ever before, the security man thought. But then, Galloway thought, I suppose you had better never lose that *edge*, that hyperawareness.

No matter what the techs at the sensors said about the air and gravity and so on, there were always surprises. *Always*. The smell, the taste of the air, the gravity, bugs, noises, the "feel" of a planet were *always* different from what you thought they would be. Galloway shrugged, mentally. He'd been born and raised in the light gravity of Mars, and to him *Earth* was strange and exotic. It was only through constant exercise to strengthen his muscles, to be able to withstand the much higher gravity of Earth, that he had been able to enter and graduate from Starfleet Security Forces School.

One thing the instructors there had taught him: Watch your commanding officer like a hawk. "Watch out for the glory-seekers," old Sergeant-Major Workman had told them. "Watch out for the ones who think the new mudball is just like where they grew up. Watch out for the young princes and nobles from some of those two-by-four kingdoms—they might have gotten through the Academy but they still think other lifeforms should obey orders. Watch out for the Oh-look-at-the-wonder-of-it-all types. They'll lead you right into a swamp or some kind of energy drain or something. And watch out for the xenophobes! They're the kind that will blast anything that doesn't have two legs, two arms, and speak Universal-English."

Franson, the one-armed, one-legged lesson in what not to do, had told them, "Don't think all officers are thickheads, because they aren't. You don't buy commissions in Starfleet, you earn them. But there are some who think they know everything, know so much they've lost all practical sense at all. Look at me. I had a young lieutenant who thought a Rigellian shocker-worm was safe because it was pretty."

Galloway kept an eye on Lieutenant Commander

Chekov. It was Galloway's first tour on the *Enterprise*, but he'd seen Chekov's type before, on the *Leo*, the *Jassan*, the *Nelson*, that sharp young Loot First who had been on the *Thelonii*, the one who thought his speed and accuracy with a phaser was all anyone needed. Ambitious, eager for adventure, eager to prove himself or herself against Nature, the Universe and the Laws of Probability.

"Sir," the transporter chief said, and Chekov motioned Galloway and the four others forward. They stepped up onto the focusing disks on the transporter stage. A little tense, Chekov nodded to the transporter chief.

Galloway heard the rising whine and felt the strange, not unpleasant sensation of the electronic scan of his body. The transporter room flickered and fragmented before him and the red sky of Kappa Rho IV dissolved in. The drag of the heavier gravity almost knocked him to his knees, but Galloway stiffened his legs and took it. He would never give in, never let any planet defeat him, not unless it defeated the others first.

Chekov switched on his tricorder and did a sweep, walking around the weapons-ready group, aiming outward. That gave Galloway time to adjust to the crushing gravity. It seemed to affect the others, too, as they moved slower, but to Martian-born Galloway, it was torture.

The planet was grim. A red-giant sun bathed everything in crimson and it was oppressively hot. The ground was gray, with purple and green-gray vegetation, small, stunted plants growing low to the rocky soil.

"Who'd ever want to live *here*?" Friedman asked.

"Quiet," Galloway said easily. He was listening. The winds were strong, gusting and lessening. Far off he could see a sandstorm boiling into the atmosphere. He took a few steps toward the edge of the hilltop which had been their vantage-point landing focus and saw a wide stretch of gray-green valley and a trace of something shiny which could have been a stream.

"I don't think anyone wants to live here," Chekov said, putting his tricorder back. "But we have to assess it, add it to the preliminary survey charts."

Friedman nodded. "They can't all be like Mura, huh, Commander?" Myra had been a lush, semitropical planet with great oceans, a million islands, and a native humanoid race who thought the people from the stars were gods.

Chekov smiled and pulled out his communicator, flipping it open. "*Enterprise*, this is Chekov."

"*Mister Chekov*," Spock answered.

"Preliminary survey report, sir. Gravity one point eight four two as expected; air thick and hot but breathable; but it's an inhospitable place, sir."

"*Oh?*" Spock responded, and Chekov remembered that the planct Vulcan's mean temperature was 140 degrees and that to many, this planet would seem like a winter wonderland, compared with Vulcan. "*Proceed, Mister Chekov. Report back in one hour.*"

"Aye, sir. Chekov out." He pointed toward the valley. "Let's go."

Galloway led them down over the sharp stones and around the long-thorned plants until they were on the flatland, where Chekov called a rest. Everyone was sweating, uncomfortable, and exhausted from the gravity, which was more than three-quarters more than Earth's. But to Galloway it was several times the gravity to which he had been born. His face was drawn but he kept the same stern, impassive face he always did. No one was going to know he was all but ready to collapse. Coming down the hill had been like carrying several men on his back.

Chekov checked the samples which two of the security men had been charged with gathering: a snip of thornbush, several rock samples, an armored beetle, still rolled up in a defensive ball, and a flask of air.

The Russian-born officer looked at the beetle carefully. Nature had so many methods of self-protection: camouflage, scales, teeth, claws, imitation and mimicry, muscles. This bug could be swallowed and pass right through its predator and unroll later and go on about its business with only a short interruption in its life.

Chekov thought about the pretty, inoffensive-looking Eminiar Fifth Column arachnid. Its method of obtaining food was to sit in some exposed position, its fiery-ed cilia waving in the breeze until it was attacked. It would then fold itself into a tight knot of overlapping chitin plates, coated with an acid-resistant gel, and let itself be swallowed.

Once inside the one who had eaten it, it expanded, stuck out legs to prevent regurgitation, then ate its way to the creature's heart, guided by the vibrations. It then used the corpse to lay eggs and to feed itself until the eggs were hatched.

A grim but violent reminder that everything pretty is not safe, Chekov thought.

"All right," he said, motioning them on. At the end of the hour he contacted the Enterprise again. "Frankly, Mister Spock, the mineral content here is low. Very little iron. The heavy gravity simply comes from a *lot* of rock."

"Not exactly a technical analysis, Mister Chekov, but accurate enough in its way. Continue for another hour. Lieutenant Nakashima in the other hemisphere reports similar findings."

"Aye, sir. Chekov out."

He motioned to Galloway, who got the exhausted security men to their feet. They crossed the valley and with great effort scaled the low hills on the north. Galloway, in the lead, was the first to find the next thing of interest.

There was a wide, low cave, and a scuffed flat area before it. Bones of animals and pits of some kind of fruit or vegetable littered the perimeter, forming an almost defensive fence. "Careful," Galloway cautioned, his phaser in his hand.

"Phasers on Stun," Chekov ordered. Galloway gave him a dark look. Sometimes stunning worked, but with certain creatures with a different nervous system it only irritated them, made them angry. But he turned his phaser to Stun and stepped over the bone "fence."

It came out of the cave like a striking snake. One long lunge, going straight for Galloway's legs. He fired and the creature jerked, but his mouth still clamped over Galloway's left leg. Five other phasers struck it at that moment and the creature released him, screaming in a thin, high cry.

It was wide and long, a doubled whip of muscle, something like a paired snake. Its tail was as big as a Terran alligator, only smooth, gray, and mottled. It twisted and the tail knocked Lieutenant Commander Chekov off his feet and against a rock. Then it bolted straight back into the cave.

Chekov rose shakily, struggling against pain, exhaustion, and the gravity of Kappa Rho IV. He went at once to where they had laid out Galloway. He was bleeding from lacerations, but his tough Starfleet boot had protected him fairly well. Chekov reached for his communicator, to have them beamed up, but he pulled forth a handful of shattered parts. Even then they might have patched the molecular blocks together, but another one had been ripped loose and lost somewhere in the dirt.

"That's all right," Chekov said. "Less than an hour, they'll miss our report and come for us." Galloway couldn't help glowering, as the communicators were usually not issued to "mere" security personnel. But Friedman had bandaged his leg with a medical spray, and at least he'd get off this accursed planet where he weighed several times his "real" weight.

"As long as that whatever-it-as wasn't lethal," Galloway reminded Chekov as Friedman gave him a booster shot of Omni-immunizer.

"We'll just wait," Chekov said.

The trouble was, the *whatever-it-was* had friends. They came slithering out of caves all over the hill, rippling over the boulders and rocks, wide jaws spreading, coming with a speed which seemed incredible, considering the gravity.

"Phasers on Kill," Chekov ordered. The security men formed a ring, firing with great accuracy, disintegrating the whatever-snakes right and left.

"I feel like General Custer," Galloway said, blasting one of the creatures as it launched itself from a rock.

Then, suddenly, they were gone. A few slithering sounds, then silence. "We've beaten them," Friedman said happily. Galloway looked at him with disgust.

"Haven't you ever heard of regrouping your forces?"

"You mean, uh, they'll come again?"

"Friedman, anything which attacks as vigorously as they did will attack again. This time, probably from a different angle."

Chekov looked thoughtful for a moment. "Friedman, put Sergeant Galloway up on that rock, the highest one. Quickly!"

"Yes, sir!" Friedman responded.

"Hey, what—"

"Quickly!" Chekov snapped. He pointed at the others. "Get up on a rock. The bigger the better! Move!"

"What's he up to?" Friedman whispered to Galloway as they shoved him up on a large boulder, sweating and grunting. It was like lifting a safe.

"I don't know, maybe he—"

The ground erupted. The whatever-snakes twisted into the air, dirt flying, their tails slashing back and forth before they fell into the hole they had dug in the midst of the party's area. A boulder tipped and rolled over. A snake's sharp teeth clamped on the lower left leg of one of the men who had lifted Galloway up. Friedman couldn't fire, for the phaser would also disintegrate the man, who was too tightly in contact. He fumbled at switching to Stun, and Chekov beat him to it.

The whatever-snake reared back, releasing the security man, and Galloway himself disintegrated the beast. The large rock upon which Chekov stood was undermined and started to roll. The Starfleet officer ran over the rolling rock much like a logger might, and leaped to another rock.

Dirt, rocks, boulders toppled into the hole carved out beneath them by the savage snakes. Another boulder shook and a security man lost his balance and sprawled, falling with a scream into the churning pit, the boulder rolling on top of him.

Friedman scrambled up, slipped and fell to the ground at the edge of the newly formed pit. He caught his balance and dodged between rocks just as a whatever-snake struck at him. He clawed his way up Galloway's boulder and started to help him off.

"No," the sergeant growled. Laboriously he got up on one elbow and fired with deliberate speed into the boiling snake pit below him, disintegrating one after another of the creatures.

Chekov added his fire to that of Galloway, aiming at keeping the thick-bodied creatures away from undermining the boulder on which Galloway rested.

Then there was a flurry of activity in the pit and spumes of dirt shot into the air, falling swiftly to the ground as the snakes tunneled into the soil and got away.

A long moment of silence followed, and then Galloway let out a long sigh. He looked at Chekov with new respect. The officer hadn't panicked—he'd out-thought the vicious creatures and saved them all. But the Russian officer looked worried. "Sir?"

"Yes, Galloway?"

"What's the matter? Do you think they'll return?"

"I don't know, but . . ." Chekov hesitated. "Suppose those were intelligent life?"

Galloway blinked. The whatever-snakes *had* been quite shrewd in their unusual mass attack, but that didn't make them *intelligent*. Intelligent creatures— self-aware minds—had a special status in Federation rules. The Prime Directive said Starfleet representatives were not to interfere. Yet surely it might be taken into account they were attacked first.

But then, Galloway knew, those admirals and politicians back on Earth and in the Grand Council take a different, "broader" view. Not being on the ground, as it were, they could hold more easily to the lofty ideals of noninterference. But when something tries to eat you, you fight back as best you can and you don't ask it to take a Federation intelligence test as it's trying to pull you into its lair.

His leg throbbed, but he ordered Friedman to take care of the other man who had been bitten. He looked at Chekov and saw the dark-haired young officer look at his watch. "Think it's all right to get off the rocks?" he asked.

Chekov shook his head. "Let's just stay here. We have two wounded and nothing to prove by going on."

"One thing, sir," Galloway said, and Chekov looked at him.

"Whether those snakes were intelligent or not."

"Hey, Sarge," Friedman complained, looking up from the leg he was spraying. "How you gonna prove that one way or another?"

"No, he's right," Chekov said. "We have about twenty minutes . . . they'll miss us and do a scan and probably transport down another team."

Galloway groaned. Glaser had the reserve duty; he'd just love to rescue Galloway. But twenty minutes could be a lifetime, he thought—or what was left of one. What would those snakes try next?

"I think I have the test," Chekov said from atop his rock. "The trouble is, if the snakes pass it we might have some serious trouble."

So they sat and waited. Chekov explained his idea, but no one commented except Galloway, who was really only being polite. "Sounds reasonable to me, Commander."

It was hot, they were tired, sweaty, exhausted, their breathing labored, and their bodies like lead. Chekov kept an eye across the valley, and when he saw the sparkle of six columns of light, he stood up and waved.

Spock raised one eybrow. "And what was this test of intelligence of yours, Mister Chekov?"

"Well, sir, there are a lot of animals in the galaxy who attack on sight, no doubt of that. To defend territory or family, to get food or to defend food. But they have no egos, which is a function of intelligence and self-awareness."

Spock said nothing, patient with the obvious. "If hurt, an animal might attack and attack again. But on the whole nonselfaware creatures will run when they are attacked or hurt. When we encountered the first whatever-snake we were invading its territory. When they attacked in concert it was to defend territory . . . and possibly for food, too. So if they attacked *another* time it was a function of some kind of intelligence."

"And if they *didn't* attack because they had reasoned out it was futile?"

Chekov grinned slyly. "Then they would be of a high enough intelligence for us not to bother them again."

"Seems to me you win either way, Mister Chekov. They don't attack, you're saved and they are intelligent; they *do* attack and they are intelligent. That is not problem-solving, Mister Chekov."

"No, sir—but it is survival."

"Granted. What will your recommendation be, then?"

"Unsuitable planet for colonization; too hot, gravity more than recommended limits, and hostile, possibly intelligent life forms."

"Mister Nakashima agrees. Log it."

"Yes, sir!" Chekov turned to leave, and Spock stopped him.

"Mister Chekov, in the future, please observe the more standard forms of intelligence determination."

"I will if I can, Mister Spock, I will if I can."

To Wherever

Montgomery Scott regarded his precious warp drive engines with a serene pleasure. They were running smoothly, producing the power which sent the U.S.S. *Enterprise* to wherever Admiral Kirk wanted to go.

Scott smiled softly, his thick black moustache turning up slightly. *To wherever they wanted to go.* Theoretically there was no limit to how far the *Enterprise*, or any other Federation starship, could travel, given enough fuel.

Across the galaxy. To another galaxy. The sky was *filled* with galaxies. Hundreds, thousands, *millions* of them! Not stars, but *galaxies*. Each galaxy with its hundreds of millions of stars, and most of the stars with planets.

The concept was almost too large for anyone to grasp, and perhaps no one could, completely. True, the great starships *could* travel to distant galaxies, but even to the nearest, either of the Magellanic Clouds—two small galaxies orbiting the Milky Way galaxy—was 160,000 light years. The crew would be considerably aged, even at warp speeds. And the next nearest, the beautiful spiral of Andromeda, was twelve times further, about 2.2 million light years. Astronomers estimate that galaxy to have 300 billion stars.

So, thought Scott, for all practical purposes we can't go *everywhere*, but we can darn near go anywhere. Certainly in our "home" galaxy. All we have to do is want to bad enough, and we can go, making the sacrifices needed.

His proud smile widened. Warp drive, the "magic" drive that broke mankind free of the isolation of a single, rather minor star system, and sent its sons and daughters flying out to meet the wonders of space.

Infinite diversity in infinite combinations, as the Vulcans say. And my engines are what make it possible, Scott thought. With only impulse engines we'd spend half our lives just getting from Earth to Sigma-14, where the *Enterprise* was presently heading. They were fine engines for orbiting a planet, or for slight trips and delicate manuevers, but they didn't have "legs."

"Mister Scott," a crewman said.

"Yes, Heineman?" The Chief Engineer said, turning toward the young Specialist-First.

The engineer pointed at a read-out panel and Scott frowned. Only .003 off norm, but at light speeds everything was exaggerated and made potentially more explosive.

"Computer Analysis, Mister Heineman," Scott snapped. The youth turned and his lean fingers stabbed at a button panel. Two screens popped into life and figures marched up them. "Put it in graph form," Scotty ordered.

The lines rose and fell and his frown deepened. "Give it a future," he said, and the technician extended the trends. If no factors were changed this was the way it would be in one standard hour, in two, in eight, in twenty.

"Trim the sine curve," Scott said, his own strong fingers dancing across a computer keyboard. Heineman punched out a graphic display and they stared at it. The time was extended, the severity lessened, but only slightly. "Security check," Scott ordered, and several of the engine room crew went quickly to work at making certain the information being fed to the read-out screens was correct.

Scott sat down in one of the chairs before the computer terminal, his hand rubbing thoughtfully at his face as each of his assistants reported back that all information was within one-thousandths of a percent correct.

The integrated matter and antimatter balances

were correct, in fact were right on the Cochrane curve. The annihilation of the dual matter was what created the fantastic power that the warp drive engines needed. But Scott felt in his bones that something was very wrong. He shifted uneasily in his seat, his mind racing through all the areas and processes needed.

In the days of the Industrial Revolution and ever since there existed a breed of men to whom engines—whether steam-powered, electric, or electronic—were living things. They knew the *sounds*, the vibrations, the click and clatter and hum, the heat and pressure and radiation. When something was wrong, they knew it, and often before gauges or dials or read-out panels told them.

There was only one way to find the exact flaw and fix it. Shut down the engines, then individually test each component and process. Scott stood up. This was not something he could handle over an intercom. "Mister Heineman, you have the conn," he said, and strode from the engine room.

Heineman looked at the others. They looked as worried as he felt, yet none of them could tell why. Heineman smiled ruefully; it was a bit like having a dog who was barking or whining yet its owner could not yet tell why.

As the hum of the engine room faded and the turbolift took Scott to the deck which housed the captain's cabin, Scott reviewed the way he should tell Captain Kirk. Straight out, of course, there was no other way. But he thought about how much James Kirk knew about the engines which drove the mighty *Enterprise.*

Oh, he knew the principles, the positive and negative atoms destroying each other and creating vast power under controlled conditions. He knew that his captain's true role was not in understanding the minute details of the ship's operations, but in understanding the people who did know, and in understanding what both ship and crew were capable of.

The turbolift stopped and the doors hissed open. Scott stepped out, a frown still creasing his forehead. "Ah, Mister Scott." He turned at the familiar sound of the first officer's voice.

"Mister Spock," he said to the Vulcan.

"Mister Scott, did you hear? Starfleet reported an energy wave proceeding toward the Andromeda galaxy from the exact point in space where V'ger seemed to dissolve."

"Hmm? That's nice," Scott said, looking thoughtfully down the corridor toward Captain Kirk's quarters.

"Nice?" Spock's slanted eyebrows angled ever more sharply. "One of the strangest and greatest constructs in the history of several races turns to energy, energy with a *direction,* and you find it 'nice'?"

"Eh? What's that, Mister Spock?"

The Vulcan eyed him speculatively. "Mister Scott, what is the difficulty? Is there anything I might do?"

Scott pulled his attention away from the hall and

looked at the tall, lean first officer, recalling that Spock was also the Science Officer, someone with a wider ranging knowledge of science than his own. "You're agonna call me strange, Mister Spock, but I have me a feeling."

"Go on, Mister Scott. You are hardly known to be given to flights of wild imagination."

"It's the matter-antimatter pods, Mister Spock. They're only point zero-zero-three, but I ran a projection. Even with some trimming and adjustment they will be moving into the red within forty hours."

"What's wrong? Is the magnetic bottle in imbalance?" Scott shook his head. "The quality of the matter in question is satisfactory?"

"Standard Starfleet issue, sir; dilithium crystals right from the supply depot on Luna. I saw it all brought aboard myself, before we set out to stop V'ger."

"As I recall, Mister Scott, we have had considerable difficulty with dilithium crystals in the past. Could this be a recurrence of any of those problems?"

"No, no, sir," Scotty said, shaking his head doggedly. "I checked on everything but pulling the crystals myself."

"And now you want to examine the crystals themselves," Spock said, "which requires a shutdown." Scott nodded. Spock thought a moment. "I shall accompany you to the captain's quarters," he said.

Scott said, "I'd be grateful, Mister Spock."

They proceeded to Kirk's doorway and announced

themselves. "Come in," Kirk said. He was in a casual lounging robe, seated in a chair. He put down the repro copy of an early twentieth century writer, Maugham, and took off his glasses to look at the two men. "Surely things are not as grim as they seem, gentlemen?"

Scott quickly outlined the problem. "How long will we be down?" he asked.

"I don't know, sir," Scott replied. "Five hours at the minimum, if nothing is radically wrong. The TR-19 could be faulty. Or it could be the crystals themselves. Better figure eight hours."

Kirk glanced at a chronometer. "Mister Scott, we are on a tight schedule. Mister Spock, please tell him why."

"Our cargo is Melantron-114," Spock said. "It is a new drug developed by Johns Hopkins on Luna for bifetor fever." Scott's eyes widened, for the fever was deadly. "A plague is sweeping Sigma-14," he continued. "We must get there as soon as possible."

"Aye," Scott said, "but if we don't stop we won't get there at all."

"Do it, Scotty," Kirk said. "Mister Spock, inform Starfleet and the authorities at Sigma 14 of the delay. Get to it," he said.

Scott thumbed the wall communicator. "Engine Room. This is Engineer Scott. Stop all engines. Mr. Heineman, prepare to dismantle the crystal matrix!"

Scott stared at the crystal under the microscope, then shook his head. "It shouldn't be," he muttered.

"Someone must have switched shipments, or . . ." He hesitated, momentarily afraid to voice such an accusation. "Or there was some bribery involved!"

"But why?" Heineman asked. "We were certain to find out, check back, and the culprit would be caught."

"Aye, laddie," Scott said. "But if we are delayed long enough, the bifetor fever will have killed most of the population of Sigma-14."

"Who—?"

Scott pressed the communicator button. "Bridge," he told the computer.

"Yes, Mister Scott?" Spock said.

"Mister Spock, the dilithium crystals have been sabotaged. Or switched for rejects. We can't go on without risking blowing up the whole vessel!"

"I'll wake the captain," Spock said.

"We've got the impulse engines, o'course," Scott said, "but that's like trying to paddle across the Atlantic, Captain."

Kirk frowned. "Have you heard the great news, gentlemen? There's an ion storm headed this way."

"That'll disrupt everything, Captain," Scott groaned. "You never know what one of those terrible storms can do, but the least of it will be considerable on-board damage."

Spock stepped to the terminal and punched up the information, studying it for a few moments. "I don't think the impulse engines will get us out of the way, Admiral," he says. "It's a very large storm."

"And we *must* shut down?" Kirk asked Scott, who nodded, his face tense and dark. "Very well, then. Mister Scott, do what you must do, and do it quickly. Mister Spock, make the ship ready to weather the storm."

Specialist First Heineman set the casing down carefully, and another specialist tagged it. The tagging would make for quicker reconstruction later. Heineman began to unbolt the next piece of inner shell. "Mister Scott, I've . . . I've never been in an ion storm before. Uh, what can I expect?"

"Hand me that spanner. Thank you. Well, son, the one thing you can expect from an ion storm is the unexpected. Never saw two exactly alike. It's a cloud of raw energy, as ye know, but like any sample of air or water, it's always a wee bit different from any other sample. Watch it now, that plate has to be eased out of there."

"Yes, sir. But will the ship go dead or what?"

"Parts, maybe. That's it, to the left . . . ah. Theoretically, an ion storm could wreck us. Rupture the dilithium crystals, put the electronics out so badly we'd never repair, blank the library computer, all sorts of mischief."

"Sounds like more than mischief to me. I got it. Terry, take this. *Easy!* Hand me the sentrilizer. Here you are, sir."

"Aye, laddie, an ion storm is a terrible thing. Normally, o'course, you can outrun them. But now . . . we'd better hurry. Time and reality aren't quite the same in an ion storm. And there's talk of an antimatter ion storm, but that's just speculation. Watch that access plae . . ."

"Sickbay."
"Sickbay. McCoy."
"Bones, are you ready down there?"
"As ready as we'll ever be, Jim. When in the devil will Scott be finished?"
"Not in time to escape it. We'll get the fringes at the very least and probably more."
"How nice," McCoy said dryly. *"McCoy out."*
"Mister Sulu, the position of the storm?"
"Zero-Five-Nine True, sir—about six minutes until first contact."
Kirk thumbed the ship's intercom. "This is Captain Kirk. We are at Intersect minus six minutes."
Spock looked up from his station. "Interesting configuration, Admiral. A greater energy intensity than we've seen before."
"What does that mean, Spock?"
"Unknown, Admiral."
Kirk nodded as if that was the expected answer. "Batten all hatches," he murmured.
"Sir?" Sulu said, turning toward him.
"Nothing, Mister Sulu, just a very old nautical term."

Their instruments started recording electrical charges at minus five minutes, twenty seconds. At minus one minute, thirteen seconds, the readings began to vary wildly. The non-critical television circuits crackled and smeared the screens. The critical Ship's Function circuits scrambled at plus ten seconds.

"Impulse engines malfunctioning," reported Midshipman Linda Chang from the engine room. *"Commander Scott has ordered a shut-down."*

"Noted," Kirk replied, exchanging a look with Spock. The *Enterprise* now floundered within the ion storm, helpless and adrift.

At plus one minute, nine seconds the artificial gravity was temporarily rendered useless and the crew threshed about. In the control room, they clung to their seats long enough to fasten their safety belts.

At plus two minutes, four seconds the lights went out, blinked, and returned. The readings on all sensors were now so erratic as to be useless, varying wildly from zero to far beyond any normal readings. The crew clung to their bunks, seats, and posts desperately.

At plus three minutes, fifty-one seconds a photon torpedo malfunctioned and Lieutenant Lex Nakashima took emergency measures and fired it harmlessly into the storm, where its immense energy was instantly absorbed by the fiery maelstrom.

At plus four minutes, nine seconds, the antigravity went out again and stayed out. The lights went, and the separately powered emergency lights went on.

At plus four minutes, thirty-eight seconds the *Enterprise* received a severe shock, sending weightless crewmen crashing against bulkheads, decks, and overheads. Elayne Granada, the paymaster, was severely injured, as was a shuttlecraft tech.

At plus five minutes, three seconds, reality became something not quite so tangible. Friedman, a security man, saw Sergeant Galloway melt away, reforming into a rather awkwardly designed dragon. Linda Chang saw the nacelles of the ship on her screen writhe. Dr. McCoy watched in horror as his hands rippled and merged with seamless beauty into the skull of the injured paymaster.

At plus five minutes, nineteen seconds, Lieutenant Commander Chekov sensed the return of the artificial gravity and reported it to Admiral Kirk. But the gravity came back stronger than ever, going well past the Earth Norm and squashing them into their seats, gasping and trying to stay conscious.

At plus five minutes, thirty seconds, the artificial gravity snapped off and Chekov saw Alurian dancers coming out of the main screen, surrounding him, caressing him, then turning into hideous spiderlike creatures with filmy garments. He screamed and kicked loose from his seatbelt and threshed his way to the ceiling, slapping at the apparitions.

Admiral Kirk, his own perception of the bridge distorted and twisted, choked out a question in the direction of a sharp-angled blue and gray mass which was Spock at his station. "Spock! What can we do?"

The Vulcan's voice seemed to come from a great echoing distance. "I'm ... attempting ... to ...

analyze . . . the . . . storm . . . and . . . feed . . . the . . . signal . . . into . . . the . . . system . . ."

The bridge walls seemed to run like water, blurring people and instruments. Then the people seemed to stand out like sparkling columns of energy, pulsating and vibrating . . .

Beep! A humming filled the air, along with a retching stink. Sound and smell and taste and touch blurred and switched with bewildering frequency.

Beep! Words became colors and objects became sounds and smells.

Beep! Kirk thought he was going mad.

Beep! Captain . . .

Beep! Captain Kirk . . .

Beep! "Captain Kirk!"

"Yes, Sulu?" The words rolled out of his mouth like great pale balloons, floating lazily on the winds of color.

"Power restored on Secondary Circuit!"

"Spock! Power on . . ." The words ballooned and burbled as a wave of unreality overtook them. Kirk's mind flowered and grew, overcoming the ship, enveloping the great ion storm, containing it in a pocket of his mind as the rest of him searched for the meaning of life—

Beep! The wave flowed on, crashing and splattering, brining Kirk back with a rude shock to the tiny, infantile, present-mind he lived in. "—Secondary Circuit!" he finished.

Beep! Beep! Beep! Kirk identified the Computer

Malfunction alarm. He looked toward Uhura's station and saw a sleek, smooth mass of rippling brown, streaked with red and black, flowing up and over the consoles and screens. He concentrated, focused his mind and the brown liquid flowed back, took shape, and became Uhura for a brief moment, a frightened, staring Uhura, before it extended glistening brown psuedopods which burst at the ends, shooting pale brown globes into the gravityless room.

"Uhura!" Kirk gasped.

A shuddering ripple went through everything and everyone. Time seemed to run backward, like a film in reverse. The illusions repeated themselves, the apparitions reversing, running back through their own reality. Materializations faded away. Emanations died, hallucinations dissolved, phantasms drifted off.

"Solution effective," Spock said calmly.

Kirk blinked. "But the storm . . ."

"It still exists," the Vulcan officer said. "But we are innoculating ourselves continuously, as it were. Negative feedback has stabilized us, for the moment."

"How long can we last?" Kirk asked, his head still ringing with the intensity of the forced illusions. "Those illusions were pretty potent."

"They were not illusions, Admiral," Spock said, his eyes dark.

"Admiral," Sulu said.

"They were *not* illusions?" Kirk asked, staring.

"Admiral!" Chekov said urgently.

"What is it?" Kirk asked sharply. Then he saw the main screen. "Is . . . is that a malfunction?"

"No, sir," Sulu said. "I tested . . . it's what's out there."

Kirk stared, his mouth opening.

It was void. A thin gray void, colorless, yet filled with color sensed rather than seen. Immense blobs, roughly spherical, were seen in every direction, their surfaces rainbowing the colors undulating slowly across their dimpled surfaces. There were huge blobs and small blobs and medium-sized blobs, floating in the void, drifting slowly.

"What . . . what is it?" Chekov gasped. "Wha-what are they?"

"Universes," Spock said.

Those upon the bridge stared. *"Universes?"* Kirk exclaimed, voicing the incredulity of them all.

"Yes, Admiral," Spock said. "The ion storm apparently formed a breech in the reality of our universe and ejected us."

"But, sir . . ." Sulu said. "How do we . . . how do we get back?"

"Spock, how do we get back?" demanded Kirk.

"Unknown, Admiral. First we must effect repairs, although time-wise we have all the time we need."

"Mister Spock!" Uhura said. "You mean . . . outside our universe there's . . . there's no *time?*"

"Precisely, Commander."

"Spock, doesn't that mean that in our . . . our former universe great time could have passed? Eons, even," Kirk suggested.

Spock nodded. "It's possible, Admiral. There's not enough data to deduce anything. If you will give me time . . ." He stopped as the faintest of smiles crossed his lips.

But the others were too concerned with the problems of the moment. Kirk said, "That's your department, Mr. Spock." He thumbed his chair-arm controls. "Damage Control, report!"

"Preliminary, Admiral. A few broken bones and sprains when the gravity cut back in. Damage in the galley. Mister Scott reports a mess in the engine room with parts landing all over. No fatalities."

"Thank you. Kirk out." He stabbed another control. "Sickbay!"

"Doctor Chapel here."

"Where's Bones?"

"In the middle of an operation, sir. If you'll excuse me . . ."

"Of course. Kirk out. Mister Sulu, where are we?"

"Unknown, Admiral Kirk. No references. No stars, no planets, no—"

"Mister Sulu!" Kirk's voice cracked across the bridge as Sulu's voice started to rise. The young officer subsided, taking deep breaths.

"Sorry, Admiral."

"Understandable. Anyone anything to report?"

Uhura spoke up. "I think I've got our universe."

"Put it on the screen," Kirk ordered.

The scene changed. Instead of an endless spacescape of bobbling blobs there was one blob, immense and gray, with almost-seen blurs of color just under the surface. "This was nearest us, sir, just to our stern."

"How do we know if it *is* ours?" Kirk wondered aloud.

"It *was* the closest, sir," Uhura said nervously. "Sir . . . uh . . . it doesn't appear . . . um . . . as large as I thought it ought to . . . and isn't it getting smaller?"

"We are becoming larger," Spock said, looking up. "We left the universe at some speed. We retain that speed though without referents it appears we are standing still. Eventually we shall be larger than the universe we left."

Kirk stared at him, then swallowed. "How can we reverse that? We can't reenter the . . . *our* . . . universe like this! We'd wreck it!"

"I'm working on it, sir, building a computer model of where we were and what we were doing."

"But, Mister Spock," Sulu said, leaning forward. "The instruments were all reading off, way off!"

"But in a perceptible pattern, Mister Sulu. They never stopped recording, except when the power was off. Their distortions were the distortions of the ion storm, which I was recording."

"Spock," Kirk said slowly. "Are you saying you have a kind of trail back in? A reverse trail, using the decoded distortions?"

"Not exactly, Admiral, but that's close." He thumbed the ship's intercom. "Engine Room. Mister Scott?"

Aye, Mister Spock? You'll be wantin' to know how long, is that it?"

"Yes, Mister Scott. We shall need both the impulse engines and the warp drive."

"Dunno, Mister Spock, the bits and pieces are all over. I have the whole black gang picking them up. But I found the trouble. It was the dilithium crystals, sir, or one, anyway. Must have slipped past the inspectors. I'll be raisin' a bit o'Cain when we get back to Starfleet."

Kirk broke in. "Scotty, you do know where we are, don't you?"

"Oh, aye, Admiral, but I have every confidence in you and Mister Spock. We've been in this kind of trouble before and we've gotten out."

"Thank you, Mister Scott. If you will inform us the moment we have full power," Spock said. "Spock out."

Kirk rubbed a hand across his face. Scotty had referred to when a transporter had malfunctioned during a ion storm and he, Scott, McCoy, and Uhura had been sent into an alternate universe where a galactic empire existed, the mirror image of the benevolent Federation. Looking at the blobs of grayness outside, Kirk thought he understood how that could have happened: perhaps another universe had touched theirs at that precise moment and the malfunctioning transporter had sent two parties into different ships.

"Spock, do you remember how we got back from that galactic empire ship?"

"Yes, Admiral. It is on that theory I am working. In that case there were two transmitters and two receivers. In our present case, there is no receiver, so I am attempting to use the ion storm as our target and make the entire ship a transporter field."

"Can . . . can that be done?" Chekov asked.

"Given sufficient power, yes, I believe so," Spock said, his fingers on the buttons of his console. Charts, figures, columns, and calculations rolled across his screens. He seemed one with the library computer, drawing from its vast resources a hundred different bits of needed information.

The minutes passed slowly and the universe behind them seemed to shrink. The minutes became hours and the *Enterprise* was as large as the universe itself.

Chekov leaned across and whispered to Sulu. "We could come back millions of years later, you know. Billions, maybe. Maybe that universe *is* shrinking, falling back to the Cosmic Egg, to the collapse of everything, ready again for the Big Bang."

Sulu swallowed hard. "I hope you're wrong."

Chekov nodded grimly as he sat up again. "So do I."

"Bridge."

"Yes, Scotty?"

"*Ready in five minutes, more or less. New crystal in. There was nothing much wrong with the impulse engines, sir, just a blown circuit.*"

"Good, Scotty, good!" Kirk said. "Did you hear that, Mister Spock?"

The Vulcan looked briefly over and nodded his head. The long hours of calculation had wearied him, but his fingers were still calling up information, still making sense of things. "Ready in approximately six minutes, Mister Scott. We shall need full power."

"Aye, Mister Spock."

Spock looked at Kirk. "Ready, Admiral."

"Just what is it we are doing?"

"We are sitting here, once the program has started to run, and watching, sir."

"There's nothing we . . ." Kirk stopped. "It's too precise for human reactions?"

"Affirmative, Admiral. We will be backtracking, as it were. Following the precise path. I believe we will reduce in size as the gravity of our 'home' universe starts to work. When we penetrate the outer 'shell' time will start again. We shall again be in the ion storm, with all its attendant difficulties and little power left. The transporter effect will allow us to penetrate the energy balloon of the universe."

"If it is the *right* universe," Kirk said.

"Unknown, Admiral, but we will be backtracking through an essentially trackless void, with only our internal guidance system to go by."

"To the *right* universe, you hope," Uhura said with a weak smile.

"In any event, it will be our universe ever after," Spock said. "I doubt if we could recapture the precise conditions again."

Chekov gave Sulu a look and Kirk smiled faintly.

"All on one roll of the dice, then. Are you ready?" They nodded. "Battle stations!"

The klaxon sounded and ten seconds later the screens began to blink solid green. Kirk looked at Spock and nodded. "You may fire when ready, Gridley."

Spock frowned, but pressed a single control button.

They began to go back.

It took hours, for they drifted at a precise speed and direction, picking up speed as the great gray universe below them seemed to grow in size. A cheer went up when it was definitely cited as enlarging.

Time—subjective time—seemed to speed up as they plummeted toward the vast gray blob. It filled the sensor screens. They could see the rippling of colors, the non-colors, the texture of the very shell . . . it shot up at them and everyone held their breath . . . the screens went crazy, running with color and lines. The bridge elongated and contracted at the same time. Their physical reactions were fantastically swift, yet molasses slow.

Then the ion storm was battering at them.

"Stars!" Sulu screamed at the top of his voice.

The artificial gravity cut in and out. The walls distorted and twisted, but they only laughed and cheered and called out to each other. It was disorienting, horrible, frightening, and weird, but it was *their* kind of weird!

"Mister Sulu, Warp Two!" Kirk said.

"Aye, sir!"

The Enterprise pulled away. The walls returned to their usual dull conformations, the screens sobered and once again trickled figures across their faces. The floors lay flat, the hands and feet and noses of the human crew once again made sense and were where they were supposed to be.

They were out of the storm.

"Damage Control," Kirk snapped.

"Damage Control. This is Schirmeister, Admiral Kirk. It looks like we came through just fine, sir. Minor damage only."

"Good! Kirk out." He looked at Spock with a wide smile. "Well, Mister Spock, you saved us again!"

Spock raised his eyebrows. "Does that surprise you, Admiral?"

Kirk laughed. "No, Mister Spock, that does not surprise me. Not any longer. You'd only surprise me if you failed."

"Then I am to assume, Captain, that a comfortable dullness would be an admirable state."

"Well, yes, I guess you could say that."

"Fascinating," Spock said.

"Admiral, I've contacted Starfleet," Uhura reported.

"Our Starfleet?" Kirk asked anxiously. "Are we back in the same time?"

"Yes, sir. Their signal is weak and breaking up because of the ion storm, but I've checked. We're home!"

More cheers went up all over the ship. Kirk

thumbed the intercom. "This is the captain. We are going to have a homecoming party and I'm buying!"

In the engine room Montgomery Scott wiped his hands on a bit of waste, then rinsed them off in the sonic wash. He was quiet and tired. Leaving Heineman in charge he took a turbolift to E Deck, and walked along until he came to a port.

It wasn't a screen, but an actual glass-steel window looking out at the stars. He drank in their multicolored beauty until he was almost giddy.

My engines, he thought. *They brought us back, back from further than man had ever gone.*

My ship, my people, my stars.

Montgomery Scott felt very good . . . and very tired. Aloud he said, "As Mister Spock might say, fascinating."

Scott walked away, back toward his quarters, a good drink, and a comfortable bed. "Universes," he muttered. "*Universes! Plural!*"

THE END